Scorpio's Child

Scorpio's Child

Kezi Matthews

Cricket Books
Chicago

And the truth shall make you free.

—John 8:32

With appreciation and thanks to my editor, Deborah Vetter.
Every writer should be so lucky!

Library of Congress Cataloging-in-Publication Data

Matthews, Kezi.
   Scorpio's child / Kezi Matthews.—1st ed.
     p. cm.
   Summary: When a strangely behaving uncle she has never heard
of comes to live in her family's house in a small South Carolina town,
fourteen-year-old Afton, grieving over her brother's death in World
War II, tries to unravel the secrets her mother refuses to share with her.
   ISBN 0-8126-2890-X (cloth)
   [1. Secrets—Fiction. 2. Brothers and sisters—Fiction. 3. Family
problems—Fiction. 4. Grief—Fiction. 5. City and town life—South
Carolina—Fiction. 6. South Carolina—Fiction.]   I. Title.
   PZ7.M43365 Sc 2001
   [Fic]—dc21

2001028871

For Ruby
1910–1995

And for Cardell always

Scorpio's Child

June 1947

Sun in Scorpio

You are resistant to imposed change of any kind, and while you may not be openly combative, you will doggedly stand your ground.

Moon in Aquarius

Your reactions to life situations are lightning quick, coming from powerful flashes of intuition and your own fixed attitudes about how things should be. Your key to harmonious relationships lies in your willingness to be flexible and adaptive.

Scorpio Rising

You are far more stubborn than you appear to be on the surface. As long as there is a remote chance of reaching your objective, you will push on long after others have given up.

UNCLE BAILEY—*Thursday, June 12th*

*T*he back bedroom door, the door to Francis's room, closes just as Deenie and I reach the landing of the upstairs hallway.

"That him?" she whispers.

I give her a hush sign and motion her down to my room. Inside, I ease the door shut behind us. The room is filled with the shimmery glow of twilight and the velvety sweet scent of the huge magnolia tree that shades the front lawn. I snap on the table lamp next to my bed.

Deenie plops herself and her fat Manila envelope stuffed with astrology paraphernalia on the bed, kicks off her loafers, peels off her socks, and wiggles her toes up at me. Her toenails gleam like iridescent rubies. Her mother's forbidden her to use Persian Delight nail polish on her hands, but apparently toes haven't been mentioned. In Deenie's world loopholes rule—she's been walking around with outlaw toenails in her shoes and loving every minute of it.

"What happens when you wear your new sandals?" I ask.

"I guess my big red toenails'll be sticking out." She turned fifteen last week and is feeling pretty biggity.

She's been my best friend since second grade, when her father, Carter Mason, bought the *Gillford Herald* and moved back here in 1939 with his California wife and daughter.

That first day in class everybody crowded around Deenie, wanting to know all about Shirley Temple. She told us that Shirley wasn't a child at all, but a midget who smoked and drank and had been caught more than once playing cards. Gillford's own Shirley look-alike, Alicia Metcalf, made such a spectacle of herself, hollering and carrying on, that her mother had to be called to come and calm her down. Mrs. Metcalf still hasn't forgiven Deenie for breaking Alicia's heart.

"So?" Deenie's propped up against the eyelet pillow sham, fingers laced behind her head, waiting for me to tell her about *him.* I hardly know how to start.

I see him sitting at the kitchen table with Mama when I get home from school. They're drinking coffee. They're looking funny like some connecting piece is missing. Mama says, "There she is now," as I walk in on them. Then she says, "Afton, this is your uncle Bailey." I stand stock-still, staring at him. She looks slightly flustered. "My brother, Bailey. Your uncle."

"Hey," I say.

He nods, and his shoes squeak against the lino-leum under the table. Mama reaches over and touches his hand as she says, "Bailey is staying with us for a little while."

I think I'm smiling, but I'm not sure. Have I ever heard of an Uncle Bailey before? Mama is giving me a *look*.

Bailey sees it, sets his cup on the table, and without looking at me, says in a soft, raspy voice, "Hope I'm not intruding, Afton." It sounds like an apology and brings me up short. I take a good look at him. Yes, he's definitely Mama's kin with his dark blond hair, even features, and slightly squinting eyes. I look like my father, with black curly hair, gray eyes, and what he calls the Dupree dimples.

"Gee, no," I say. "This house is deader than a door-nail when Daddy's gone—you know, asailing." Neither of them says a word. "Across the briny deep?" I think I'm being cute, but nobody smiles. I flush and turn toward the refrigerator behind him, then glance back at Mama and ask, "Any lemonade left?" She gives me the *look* again. I notice a trickle of sweat curling around the back of his ear and inching down toward his sunburned neck.

He stands, towering over me. His lanky frame hangs together too loosely, and he smells different—not bad, just unfamiliar. His rumpled khaki pants bag at the knees, and his blue chambray shirt, its sleeves rolled to his elbows, is stained with wet patches at the underarms.

"Why don't I give y'all some talking room?" he says and heads for the screen door, walking as though his feet hurt. He glances at me as he passes and quickly looks away.

DEENIE LEANS FORWARD. "What'd she say when he left?" Her eyes have that slightly crossed look they get when she's concentrating.

"She said I embarrassed her."

"I mean about him. Where'd he come from?"

"I don't know. Arkansas, I guess. That's where Mama grew up."

Deenie waits for more.

"She said he's been through an ordeal and to just make him welcome without a lot of silly questions."

"What kind of ordeal?"

"Deenie! Didn't I just say I didn't know! I tried to ask her later, but she sidestepped the whole thing. She said, 'Just be nice, Afton.' "

"Hmm, when's his birthday? Maybe I can get a bead on him."

"Why would she spring him on me like this?"

"What're you so mad about?" She leans forward, scrutinizing my face. "Maybe he just decided to drop in."

"I'm not mad!"

"I know you . . . you're dagger-eyed mad, Afton."

"What?"

"Your eyes . . . when you get mad . . . they look just like two dagger points. I'll bet that's a double Scorpio thing." She rummages around in her Manila envelope, pulls out a little notebook, and begins scribbling.

"Will you stop that! She put him in Francis's room, Deenie. *Francis's* room." I sit on the side of the bed. "Something else, too. Just that fast, I didn't like him. Call it whatever you want to, but he gives me a funny, sinking feeling in the pit of my stomach."

Deenie glances at me. "Well, Gloria Starlight says always look to the moon sign for inside emotions—and your moon *is* in Aquarius." She's talking about one of her astrology idols, and I can't believe she doesn't know how stupid it sounds.

"You probably picked up some radio waves," she says. I give her an irritated look.

"Go ahead, glare," she says, "but it won't change the fact that Aquarius deals with stuff like that. The guy who came up with the walkie-talkie? Probably an Aquarian." Probably this—probably that—geez. I decide to just let it go.

Deenie taps her pencil against her notebook as she studies her ruby red toenails, then she finally says, "Find out his birthday, and I'll tell you everything you want to know." She's looking so serious, like she just discovered the cure for polio, and I burst out laughing. But this is not funny at all. Mama was looking at him in that soft way she used to look at Francis. She never looks at me that way. How come he's popped up like this all of a sudden?

The Buoy Bell—*Saturday, June 14th*

I know I'm dreaming; it's like watching a movie through a kaleidoscope where everything keeps shifting and turning. I see myself going about my business, not the least bit aware that something is moving toward me, that something in my life is changing.

Inside my dream the world is abloom with great tethered clouds of azaleas and roses, their pinks, lavenders, and yellows shimmering through a brilliant morning sunlight that spills over rooftops and down lawns. A whirring noise grows louder. Overhead an agitated cloud forms and hovers over Hudson's Drug Store. As I watch, it turns into a silvery bus and slowly descends to the street, leaving a bruised stain in the sky.

The front door of the dream bus swings open, and the driver holds up a sign. I can't read it at first, then I see that it says: *This is where you get off.* One second, the people inside the bus are bunching up in the aisle pushing toward the front. The next second, they're inside Hudson's Drug Store crowding around the lunch counter, smiling and talking as if they're all longtime friends. Someone says, "Where's that man?" They all turn and stare out the plate-glass window toward the bus. An old woman in a country dress made of flour sacks with a sunbonnet shading her face shakes her head and says, "He be lookin' like trouble to me."

The man is sitting at the rear of the bus, staring back at the people. His face has a strange, frozen look to it. Then I realize that he's really watching me, and my heart bangs against my chest.

I want to run, but my legs won't move. I'm sure something bad is about to happen. Instead, I suddenly swoosh skyward and sail across town, touching down blocks away at Gillford High. It's the last day of school, and everyone is laughing and horsing around, clearing out their lockers.

"I didn't know you could fly," Deenie says. "It must be a Scorpio trait." She writes my birth date on a blackboard in big block letters: November 4, 1932. 6:15 A.M. "Sun in Scorpio with Scorpio Rising—double trouble," she says.

The chalk marks on the blackboard expand and contract as if they're breathing.

"Why did you decide to be born then?" she asks, holding a pencil and pad like a stenographer.

I shrug. I don't know.

"You must have had a reason, Afton. Why did you pick the parents you did?"

I shrug again. I don't know.

"Well, Gloria Starlight knows," she says. "She sent this for you." She hands me a map of South Carolina like the ones they have out at Reeves Gas Station. "You get to decide which roads to take."

I open out the map and study it. "How do you and Gloria know all this?" I ask her.

She smiles, and before she can answer, I'm back in front of the drug store. The bus is gone. There's a dog coming up the street. It's a big dusty stray in off the highway—its tail hung low, its ears laid back in submission. I'm wondering if I need to be afraid of it, when the man from the bus steps out from behind a tree. He slaps his thigh, and the dog falls in behind him as they head on up the street toward the house at 329 Lilac—where I live.

Off in a far corner of my dream, I see Daddy's ship disappearing over the horizon, and I wonder anxiously who'll look out for me now. I hear the melancholy dinging of a buoy bell. It's warning me that a marker has entered my life, and things will never be the same.

TEARS ARE FALLING ON LILAC STREET—
Monday, June 16th

I can't believe she's put him in Francis's room. Did she have the right to do that? Mama, I want to scream, how could you?

There are certain days in your life when the blood on your wound remains forever fresh. On Tuesday, March 6, 1945, at 2:30 in the afternoon, I see Bobby Markham coming with the news. I watch him bank his bicycle around the corner. He doesn't have to pause and look around. He's lived in Gillford all his life. He knows who lives behind the house numbers.

Ride on by, Bobby. Don't stop here. Take it somewhere else today. But no pleading can undo this. His lips tremble. His voice falters. "Hey, Afton," he says so softly my stomach lurches. He hangs his head as he hands Mama the telegram—as he hands her all that is left of Francis, her eighteen-year-old boy, her firstborn.

Later, the yellow rectangle of paper with the white ticker-tape message glued on it sits propped up against the sugar bowl on the kitchen table. It regrets to inform us. Then we are crying and crying and crying. Mama makes not a sound. Her head is bowed—a silent flood of grief pouring from her eyes, streaming down her cheeks, dripping from her chin, disappearing into the front of her blouse. Deenie is making little monkey sounds of disbelief that catch in her throat. My tears are swirling inside my head like bits of glass, making me dizzy, and the only thing I see behind my eyes is Francis letting out his Tarzan yell as he swings across Hingle Creek on the thick towing rope Daddy knotted around the oak's huge arm. I see the rope fray and unravel.

Francis won't be coming home. Francis with his stubborn, curly hair the color of cornflakes, his loopy smile with the chipped front tooth. His last drop of blood has oozed into a soggy battlefield in Europe. I am here, breathing, my heart still pumping while Francis is—where? Not here. Never here again.

We are all crying. Mama. Deenie. Me. Auntie Mason from across the street. All up and down Lilac Street tears are falling. Throughout the house the tables and chairs, the sofa, the stacks of Superman comics waiting for him inside the hall closet, the Lucky Dog baseball glove hanging on the closet door hook, the early ruby-throated hummingbird fluttering under the eaves—crying, all crying. Somewhere out on the Atlantic, Daddy is pacing the deck of his convoy ship, restless, anxious. A sharp ache in his heart is warning him of our tears, his heart that will never mend. Even Franklin Delano Roosevelt is crying.

How can she put this strange, squinty-eyed man in Francis's room?

Don't Tell Daddy—*Wednesday, June 18th*

*Y*ou writing to Daddy?" Mama is standing in my bedroom doorway, picking with restless fingers at the frilly
gray feathers of her duster. She's flushed, almost pretty
again, her blond bangs peeping out from the silky floral
kerchief tied around her hair.

I don't bother to smile, and she knows why.
*Surprise! Here's an Uncle Bailey for you, Afton—out of the
blue, so be nice.* I just nod and look back down at the
sheet of pale blue stationery on my lap desk.

We don't know for sure where Daddy's headed
this time—either Australia or New Zealand, probably
both—but we always have to write in care of the shipping
company in Charleston. They send the crew's mail on
by air so it's waiting for them when they dock.

I wait quietly for her to go on down the hallway.

"Let's not say anything about Bailey right now,
O.K.? I don't want Charles worrying. . . ." Her voice
floats toward me, whispery and hesitant.

My scalp tightens, and I look up at her. Don't tell Daddy? As Auntie Mason likes to say, *I can smell that dead rat a block away,* and this one smells like Mama's blurred kind of lying—not an outright lie, just hiding something. She knows what I'm thinking. I can tell by the way she drops her chin and studies the duster.

"Afton," she says, "Bailey's been through so much. He needs to get on his feet."

"What's he been through?"

"A lot. His . . . his spirit is hurt." She shakes her head. When she glances up, her eyes are watery. What's going on? Ever since my monthlies started, she's always telling me I'm not a child anymore, but she still treats me like one when it suits her.

"What hurt him so bad?" I ask. I deserve to know what's going on. I deserve to know why I shouldn't tell Daddy that her brother, Bailey, is here. There must be a pretty good reason why Daddy would worry if he knew.

"Don't look at me like that," she says.

The door to Francis's room opens, followed by footsteps in the hallway.

"Morning, Barbara," he says.

It's past eleven. His eyelids are puffy from sleep. Their voices have the same whispery tone. Mama's face brightens when she looks up at him. He smiles at me in that slight, pursed-lip way strangers have.

"Bet you're good and hungry," she says to him. They chuckle softly as they head down the stairs. Bailey and Barbara. Barbara and Bailey. Sugar and spice and puppy dog tails. I'm really out of sorts.

Mama and I have already eaten breakfast, but I feel left out just the same. Couldn't she have said, "Come have a cup of coffee with us, Afton"? I wonder what Daddy had for breakfast this morning.

He's been in the merchant marines since before I was born. He likes to tell how he ran off and joined the navy when he was sixteen. He likes to say he has salt water in his veins. He tried land life after the navy, he says, but the sea kept calling him back.

He's a big man with eyes gray as storm clouds— eyes that can nail you to the floor if he's riled. His black, wavy hair is going gray at the temples now. His short-trimmed beard and the way he combs his thick hair back give him somewhat of a Jesus look. Once he opens his mouth, though, folks get past that pretty quick. He's ten years older than Mama, and this year they've been married twenty-one years.

People like to tease him, asking how come a sailing man makes his home in Gillford, sixty miles from the ocean. He says for love of a good woman. Mama says that Charleston is too much of a hubbub for her, that she was born a country girl and will die a country girl. Gillford is likely their big compromise, a sign that they want to be together in a way that suits them. But I don't think Daddy has any idea of what Mama is like when he's not home. I don't think he has any idea of her headaches, her sipping brandy, how she often holes up in the house and lives from one radio program to the next. Besides Auntie Mason and me, sometimes the only people she talks to for days on end are Isaac, who scrubs the porches, washes the windows, and mows the lawn, and his mother, Florence, who does our laundry.

But the minute that home-port phone call from Daddy comes in, she turns into this whole other person, stocking the pantry and refrigerator with all the makings for his favorite meals, sprucing herself and the house up, putting vases of flowers—oleanders, roses, cut azaleas—in the living room and up in their bedroom. She becomes Captain Charles Dupree's perfect, smiling wife, even welcoming Daddy's cronies, who gather on the porch all hours of the day and evening, enthralled with his stories.

Watching her with Daddy the last couple of years, I've started wondering what he'd think of the Barbara he leaves behind.

I ball up the sheet of stationery and aim for the wastebasket. Here I am again, going along with something that doesn't feel right. It seems like the older I get, the more she whispers in my ear, "Let's just keep this to ourselves." You'd think it would tie us close together, but it doesn't. I hate it. One of these days, I'm going to stop it—but not today. Today I won't tell Daddy about Bailey. Brother Bailey. Uncle Bailey. Strange Bailey.

LOOKING FOR HEROES—*Friday, June 20th*

Bailey's got a job at J & L Sawmill. It's just day to day doing dirty-bird work, but at least he's out of the house from six to six. I wish I knew why I feel so uneven when he's around. Deenie says it's chemistry—the same reason why I don't like mustard greens. I don't know about all that. I don't like mustard greens because they upset my stomach. She shrugs and says, "Well, isn't that chemistry?"

This afternoon, Mrs. Hudson and her daughter-in-law, Arlene, caught Mama out on the front porch, so of course, she had to invite them in. Mrs. Hudson is a sly old fox—even I know she's here on a fact-finding mission. I like her, though. Everybody knows she had her eye on Francis for her middle daughter, Cecelia, and she was truly grief-stricken over his death. She got up at his memorial service, walked down the aisle, and laid a single white rose on Mama's lap and said that Gillford would never be the same without Francis and that the Duprees' pain was Gillford's pain.

So, they're sitting here, Mrs. Hudson and Arlene, in almost identical pancake straw hats cocked down to one side. Arlene watches to see how Mrs. Hudson folds her white-gloved hands one over the other on her lap just so and then follows suit. They get rid of the chitchat pretty quickly today. Mama knows exactly what they're here for. I help her serve iced tea and sweet biscuits, then go sit on the piano bench.

Mrs. Hudson gives Arlene a flick of an eye signal and begins inching closer and closer to her target, Bailey. "How nice that your brother is visiting." Mama has tiny beads of perspiration at her hairline. I tune them out for just a second and snap back in when I hear Mama say, ". . . so kind of you, but he's been through an ordeal and needs time to himself." She's avoiding direct eye contact with them.

"Yes," says Mrs. Hudson, "so many boys went through such terrible ordeals." She takes a tiny bite from her biscuit, then a sip of iced tea. "What exactly did Bailey . . . is that it? . . . Bailey? . . . I hope he didn't lose a limb. Now that is a terrible, terrible ordeal. My boy Clifford says he can still feel his toes and even gets muscle cramps off that leg he left in the South Pacific. It wasn't anything like that, was it?"

Mama's eyelids are beginning to flutter. If you didn't know her, you'd think she was getting ready to tear up, but she's not. She's irritated. Mrs. Hudson studies her for a moment, looking for all the world like a cat that has something trapped behind the stove, then she touches her rouged cheek with one gloved hand, and her eyes widen in practiced surprise.

"Oh, my dear Lord, how insensitive can I be? I should have known from the lean, hounded look of him."

Mama looks startled. I'm all ears.

Mrs. Hudson leans toward Mama and lowers her voice. "Was he held captive during the war?"

Mama just stares at her.

"He was a prisoner of war? Oh, dear God in heaven, that would be a terrible ordeal." Mrs. Hudson shakes her head sadly. Arlene appears hypnotized.

"Was he in a military hospital? Is that where he's been since the war? Why, Lord knows no one will hold that against him. They say a lot of boys came back a little unsteady. They just need time to get ahold of everyday living again." She's throwing out one bait line after the other.

"Yes," says Mama, "he just needs some time to get on his feet." Before Mrs. Hudson can utter another word, Mama says to me, "Afton, why don't you play a nice selection for us?" Her eyes are narrowing into her flinty look; this is a command performance.

I turn and shuffle through the sheaf of music lying atop the Steinway upright. I'm a lousy pianist. I don't have the right kind of ear-and-finger coordination. I pull out the first movement of *Moonlight* Sonata—poor Beethoven, another heavy-hander making a run at him. My rendition isn't calm and dignified. It's what my music teacher, Miss Lyons, calls *ponderous*. And it seems to go on forever, even to me. When I'm done, everyone's eyes are a little out of focus, and Mrs. Hudson stands quickly, smoothing the front of her silk print dress.

"Just grand," she says. "You get better and better, Afton."

I look down at the carpet to keep from laughing.

Arlene stands up next to Mrs. Hudson, uncertain and obviously bored out of her skull. Finally she says to me, "I've been thinking about learning to play the banjo." Mrs. Hudson shoots her a surprised look.

Before I can answer, Arlene forgets about the banjo and says right out of the sugary blue, "Have you met Mrs. Graham's niece yet? Jo Helen? She's so cute. . . ."

This is definitely code for "Better keep your eye on John Howard." I smile, probably the fakiest smile of my entire life.

Mrs. Hudson gently takes Arlene's elbow and gives me her "chin up" smile. Mama's being gracious, murmuring little nothings while actually herding them out the front door.

After they leave, she complains of a terrible headache and goes upstairs to lie down. I straighten the living room, clean up the kitchen, then go sit out on the back steps. The yard is glowing in the late afternoon sun, and tiny speckles of insects are floating by on streams of heat. The air is heavy with the sweet, green smell of the vegetable garden. Everything seems to be in slow motion except my mind. My mind is wide awake.

Was Bailey a prisoner of war? Is that why he's so quiet and withdrawn most of the time? Was his ordeal so terrible he can't bring himself to talk about it? I smart under a sting of shame at the way I've been acting. I need to make a fresh start with him, nothing too obvious. He's so skittish; it'll have to be easy does it. I'll figure out a way.

PALE, UNBLINKING EYES—
Monday, June 23rd

"What're you messing around with that old dog for? If you're going to feed him, just put the pan down and leave him be."

I've spent the last ten minutes trying to lure the heap of wolf-gray fur out into the open. "He's been living under these bushes ever since Uncle Bailey showed up. He seems so tired and lost," I say, looking up at Auntie Mason.

The fragile curls held in place atop her head with pearly combs are now powder blue. Last month they had a purplish cast, and she was fit to be tied. "That Lucy is getting more addle-headed by the day," she said to Mama. "This is Wynona Thorp's rinse. It's a wiry-haired rinse for Lord's sake!"

She's eighty-nine years old and Deenie's great-grandmother. Her name is Rebecca Louise Gillford Mason, but when she reached her eighty-fifth birthday, there was an all-out shindig complete with Jimmy Rose's Country Band at Courthouse Square to celebrate her being the town's oldest resident and the last living child of its founder, Cyrus T. Gillford. The mayor called her our own beloved Auntie Mason, and it stuck.

"I've been noticing you all this last week trying to coax that old dog out. Smart as you are, hasn't it occurred to you that he's perfectly satisfied where he is long as you keep the food coming?"

"Yes'm, but . . ." I push the pan of food scraps under the bush and stand up. She's either shrinking by the day, or I'm getting taller. Mama thinks women over five five are ungainly, so I may be a disappointment to her there, too.

"No buts about it," Auntie Mason says. "That old dog's not looking for your friendship; he wants the food is all. You stop feeding him, he'll be gone." We can hear him snuffling and chewing.

"I'd just like to pat him on the head so he knows it's all right if he wants to hang around, that's all."

She loops her tiny arm through mine and steers me toward the front porch. "He's never going to trust you, Afton. Somebody that he thought loved him probably dumped him a long time ago. Or maybe somebody died, and he was left to fend for himself. From the looks of him, I expect he's learned some hard lessons about dealing with strangers. These road dogs lose all that puppy trust real fast."

"I think he might come out once he sees I mean him no harm."

"That old dog's got nothing left to give," she says and pats my arm as if to console me for being so naive.

I don't believe her. Something more than sympathy makes me look back over my shoulder. The dog is lying in the shadows with his head resting on his front paws, watching us with pale, unblinking eyes.

When we reach the porch, Auntie Mason grabs the railing and pulls herself up the three steps. If I tried to help her, chances are good that she'd slap my hand away and say something like, "Did you hear me cry for help!" Spunk runs in Deenie's family.

Mama's at the front screen door. "I just put a pan of sweet potato biscuits in the oven." She holds the door open. "What're you two up to?"

Auntie Mason says, "Is that Ella Hudson's recipe?"

Mama nods in agreement and says, "My, but your new rinse is lovely."

Auntie Mason smiles discreetly as they go inside, caught up in their polite back and forth. I stay outside sitting in Daddy's wicker rocker, and I watch the old dog watching me. He never blinks.

LOVE IT'S LIKE A LIZARD—
Thursday, June 26th

Love—it's like a lizard—it curls its tail upon its back and jumps right into your gizzard.

Auntie Mason says that old country proverb means you don't have any say-so about the insanity of your heart's longings.

I was seven when I first noticed John Howard Thompson. He was ten and running like something crazy to catch a low ground ball during recess. Just watching him, everything went haywire. My heart jumped, my hands shook, my legs turned to jelly, I couldn't think straight. Sometimes when I passed by him in the hallway going to class, I'd try to smile, but my lips would hang up on my teeth and I'd want to die.

My head's been filled up with his brick-red hair and chocolate-pudding eyes for almost eight years now. Everybody knows that we are a match waiting to happen. Only four more months before I turn fifteen;

Daddy says if I keep my grades up and my head on straight, he'll let me start dating once a week then. He means let me go out on a real date with John Howard.

But sometime within the last two weeks, along comes seventeen-year-old Jo Helen Graham from Savannah. Bad news travels fast in Gillford, and by eight-thirty this morning I know that John Howard took this Jo Helen to the movies last night to see Bob Hope and Bing Crosby in the *Road to Utopia*. They even went to Henderson's Ice Cream Emporium after the movie for banana splits.

I stay in my room and brood about it all day. Later, Mama insists I come down for supper, and like a pot of grief boiling over, I have to fight to hold back my tears right in front of Mama and Bailey.

"You haven't eaten a thing all day," she says. "You need to get something in your stomach." She reaches over and pats my arm. "It's just a phase boys go through," she says.

"A phase?" I ask.

"A phase." Her voice is firm. "She probably just turned his head."

This is supposed to make me feel better? The tears slide on down my cheeks.

"Stop all the snuffling now and eat your supper. It's not the end of the world."

It might as well be thumps my aching heart. I try to bite down on a small wedge of tomato only to have it wobble around in my mouth. I wind up swallowing it whole.

Mama says to Bailey, "She's always been one to take things too much to heart."

He doesn't even look up, just gives a soft snort as he digs into his plate of fried ham steak and macaroni salad. I feel my bile rising at his insensitivity, and all my good intentions about him disappear like cotton candy in the rain.

"You'd have to really love somebody to know how it feels," I say, shooting him a grieved look. He doesn't turn a hair. A strange expression creeps across Mama's face, and she nudges my foot under the table. We finish supper in silence.

I hate the way he eats with his head down, shoveling his food in as though he's on a timetable. When he's done, he says, "Thank you, Barbara," gets up, and heads out the back screen door. His napkin is still folded and unused next to his plate.

When I open my mouth to say something, Mama holds up her hand and says, "No, please, I have a splitting headache." Another one.

I get up all stiff necked and clear the table. I know he's been through a terrible time and hurts in ways I'll never understand, but he's so . . . awful . . . and right now, I'm wishing he were someplace else. I dry the last dish and hang up the dishtowel. I think of John Howard sitting in the dark theater with Jo Helen Graham from Savannah. Did they hold hands? I feel like I could cry all night long. Why did God decide to drop both Bailey Munroe *and* Jo Helen Graham on my head at the same time?

NIGHT WALKER—*Sunday, June 29th*

Moonlight spilling through the voile curtains at my open bedroom window throws delicate patterns across the hardwood floors and far wall. The glow is so mysterious and alive, I half expect to see some beautiful fairy tale creature step out of a corner. I sit up in bed, listening. The night air, cool and sweet from the midnight rain, whispers along my bare arms. The house should be still, sleeping, dreaming of the day when Daddy will come bounding up on the front porch, but I hear Bailey's restless footsteps again tonight. He's pacing back and forth in Francis's room as though he's measuring, cautiously counting his steps.

I finally asked Mama this morning if she hears him doing this at night. She pulled back into silence, a frown puckering her forehead. After a few minutes, she said, "He's just trying to figure out how to fit into things again. He's been through a lot." When I asked what, she gave me a look, shook her head, and said, "Why can't you ever just let things be, Afton?"

Before I could say another word, she asked, "Did you finish straightening up the living room?" Case closed. She's always had this way of cutting me off as if I'm getting too close. Too close to what, I don't know. Just too close. Now, I guess, it's too close to whatever is the matter with Bailey.

He's at it again tonight, walking back and forth, no pauses, just back and forth. Is he thinking of his ordeal? Is he reliving the terrible things he went through? The other Saturday I overheard a man out at Reeves Gas Station going on about things that happened during the war. I was eating a coconut marshmallow puff, waiting to meet up with Deenie, and this man went into such revolting detail, I got sick to my stomach. He told how his brother was captured, how he was slowly starving to death, how he ate bugs, even roaches, and mice and rats, breaking their necks and eating them raw, and snakes, too, when he could catch them. Anything to stay alive. That night I dreamed about Francis all night long, cold and hungry in his grave. Does Bailey pace back and forth to stay awake because his dreams are so horrible?

I hear Francis's door open, then click shut. Even though he's walking carefully, the rubber soles of the new work boots Mama bought for him squish softly on the waxed hallway floors and down the stairs.

He's been slipping out like this from the very first, gone for hours, coming in a little while before dawn. Later I'll hear him shaving in the bathroom while

Mama makes his breakfast. I never join them. I don't really know why—except I have this odd feeling that when I'm around, they don't say what they really want to say to each other.

I pad to the open window and pull the curtain aside just enough to see. He's standing at the end of the walkway, bathed in moonlight. He looks unreal, like a black-and-white block print from one of Daddy's books up in the attic—like a weary angel going about his business in the dead of night. The image stuns me, and when I strain forward to get a better look, it's gone. There's just Bailey standing there, looking up and down the sidewalk. He shoves his hands into his pants pockets, hunches his shoulders, and turns right onto Lilac. The shaggy shadow of the dog crawls out of the shrubbery and falls in behind him. Bailey's head droops forward, and I could swear he's measuring his steps, counting them off with each foot forward. Where does he go?

July 1947

Sun in Scorpio

You are one of the natural detectives of the zodiac. Nothing escapes your intense scrutiny.

Moon in Aquarius

You are emotionally drawn to helping those less fortunate and don't hesitate to give freely of your time and resources when moved to do so. However, you don't give your deeper affections easily.

Scorpio Rising

You are a keen observer and easily spot weaknesses in others. As a consequence, you do not allow yourself to reveal the full extent of your true feelings. Even your closest friends don't know you as well as they think they do.

THE SAVING STORM—*Friday, July 4th*

*I*t's one of those muggy, low-country mornings when the heat rides on top of a nervous undercurrent and whatever you put on wilts within minutes. The sun's white glare spreads across a cloudless sky, and every once in a while distant thunder grumbles from the east.

Deenie and I, Clarisse, Margaret, and Josie all show up at 8:30 sharp at Courthouse Square to help drape the bunting across the stage and string the red, white, and blue rolls of accordion paper on everything in sight. Mrs. Mason, Deenie's mother, is directing us. Every time thunder sounds off in the distance, she puts her hand to her throat and looks around as if a marauder is sneaking up on her. John Howard Thompson and Billy Tisdale are mowing the grass. The rest of the boys are unloading the picnic tables from the flatbed trailer of Teddy Hudson's truck. John Howard catches me looking at him and smiles. My stomach flip-flops, but I pretend I don't see him, and right away I could kick myself. I sure don't want him thinking I'm jealous of Jo Helen Graham. I decide to accidentally bump into him later.

Instead it's Carter Mason, Deenie's father, that I back into. He's taking pictures for the *Herald's* Fourth of July issue.

"Hold it right there, Afton! Look back over your shoulder." With my arms full of musty bunting, I twist my head around and squint at the camera. "Great," he says and snaps my picture.

I ball the bunting up in my arms so I don't trip on it. Mr. Mason strolls alongside me toward the stage. He has the bluest eyes you ever saw and a kind of sweet hangdog expression. All the women in town break into smiles if he so much as tips his hat and says how do.

"Looking forward to the show today?"

I nod and smile.

"The Gibson girls are doing their tap dance routine again this year, and I hear that pretty niece of Harriet Graham's is going to sing and play the guitar."

I haven't gotten much beyond "that pretty niece of Harriet Graham's" when I hear him say, "I called your mama earlier this week. We'd like to renew our respects to the Gold Star Mothers for the loss of their sons . . . Francis, Johnny Rutherford, and the Haines boy. We'll top it off with 'The Star-Spangled Banner' . . . get everybody up on their feet and ready for the games. Your uncle Bailey is invited, too, along with all the other veterans today . . . a good way for him to meet some of the other boys."

I think maybe I'll choke right there on the spot. First off, Bailey Munroe is definitely not a boy. And second, Daddy's at sea this summer, and without him as her buffer, even though she's a Gold Star Mother, Mama would only show up with Auntie Mason because there's no way out for her. But I know without a doubt that she won't have Bailey with her. He's too skittish and shy; wild horses couldn't drag him up on that stage.

"I'm looking forward to meeting him," says Mr. Mason. "He probably has some interesting war stories for us . . . personal experiences."

"He's . . . he's been through . . . some terrible things . . . ," I stammer. I have Mr. Mason's full attention, like white on rice. "But he doesn't talk about all that . . . stuff," I add quickly, picking up my pace toward the stage. Deenie is watching us and starts down the stage steps to my rescue.

She runs over and strikes a cutie-pie hand-on-hip pose for his camera. "How's this one, Daddy? Editor's daughter makes front page!"

He cocks an eyebrow and shakes his head. Teddy Hudson huffs and puffs over to him, and Deenie and I make our escape.

IT'S JUST PAST ONE-THIRTY, and the sky has turned a deep gunmetal gray. The sun disappeared around eleven. When the air took on that first odd metallic whiff of a summer storm heading our way, everyone at Courthouse Square started wondering if the Fourth was going to be a washout, then some of us cut out to go home for lunch.

The house is quiet and gloomy looking inside—Mama's already turned off all the lights except in the kitchen. I'm not really hungry, but I reach into the refrigerator for a chicken wing from last night's supper. One bite does it.

The weather has my skin prickly and my nerves jumpy. Thunder is rolling closer to town by the minute, and I hear Mama upstairs closing windows. Then the full wrath of it is upon us, sounding as if the roof of the world is collapsing. There's a slight pause, then thunder cracks so hard the house shakes, the kitchen light dims, and a torrent of furious rain plunges from the sky. I race to shut the kitchen windows and watch helplessly as the savage downpour flattens the row of sunflowers along the back fence. It's raining harder than the ground can absorb it, and water is pooling around the back steps.

I don't see Bailey on the back porch until he rises, barefoot, from the glider and slowly unbuttons his shirt. He flings it aside and steps off the porch into water that splashes over his feet, and he lifts his face to the driving rain. A flash of lightning fills the yard with an eerie white light, disappears, and an earsplitting crack of thunder shakes the house so hard again, my teeth vibrate. He stands there with his eyes closed, holding his arms straight up as if beseeching heaven for something. I'm sure my hair must be standing on end. I turn when Mama comes into the kitchen.

"He's out there," I say.

She peers through the window. "He's always loved storms. From the time we were children."

"But he could get hurt!"

She shakes her head, still watching him. "He can't get hurt any more than he already is."

"Mama! He could get killed!"

She seems so matter of fact. "He's probably already done that . . . more than once." I'm not sure what she means. The phone rings, and I start for it. She puts her hand on my arm. "You know better than to answer the telephone during a storm."

I look at her carefully. Don't answer the phone, but leave Bailey standing out in a thunder-and-lightning storm? She doesn't let go of my arm until the phone stops ringing.

When the rain finally starts to slacken off, he comes in and stands just inside the door dripping strings of water onto the linoleum. There's a big ridge of a scar across his chest, and I wonder how anyone could survive being hurt like that. His hair is plastered to his head, and the first real smile I've seen on his face frames crooked, stained teeth. Before Mama wraps a bath towel around his shoulders, I notice more scars, a network of small ones crisscrossing his back. He glances at me.

"It makes you feel clean," he says in his raspy, stiff voice. "The rain, it makes you feel clean."

Mama reaches up and hugs him. "Remember that storm where you lit out across the field after Bessie's calf?" Her eyes are shining. As far as they're concerned, I might as well not even be here.

I feel as though I'm watching one of those movies where you can't figure out what's going on. All I know for sure is that this storm is a gift from God to Mama—

canceling out the Fourth of July at Gillford's
Courthouse Square.

PEARL ANN—*Monday, July 7th*

Why does Bailey seem to hide from me whenever Mama goes somewhere? She's made one of her rare trips downtown to the sale at Butler's Department Store with Auntie Mason. Operation is down at the sawmill today, and Bailey is up in Francis's room behind closed doors.

I'm supposed to be inside dusting everything that isn't moving, but I'm on the front porch with Deenie's astrology magazine. "Read that article about Scorpio on page thirty-two," she said. "It's you to a T." Mama won't tolerate this kind of stuff in her house. "It's heathen," she says, but I read it anyway because every once in a while, there's a sentence or two that's so true about me, I go over it four or five times to make sure I'm reading it right. But I never let on to Deenie. She'd drive me nuts with it.

I glance up when Mr. Anderson, the mailman, turns the corner. He waves and walks on by—no mail from Daddy yet. Half a block behind him, tiny Pearl Ann Wayland is coming up the street. What's she doing so far over on this side of town all by herself? As she comes closer, I'm pretending to read, but I'm watching every twitchy little move she makes.

She is one sorry-looking child, rail skinny, hair thin and wispy as dandelion fluff. She has to be five or six by now, but she never seems to grow. Sometimes, when you see her in the wintertime, it's startling—her blue veins running like threads beneath her transparent skin, her bony arms and legs so flimsy it seems that the only thing holding her together is your eyes. Nobody knows who Pearl Ann's daddy is. Folks say even her mama, Nona Wayland, probably doesn't know.

She stops in front of the Gerards' house, staring at something in the bed of pansies. Probably one of Snowball's kittens. She squats down carefully so as not to scare it off. When she straightens up, she has a tiny garden snake dangling from one hand. Now she's stroking its head and talking to it. She hasn't seen me, and she's wrapping the little snake around her wrist as she comes on down the street. The sunlight is turning her flyaway hair silvery, making her look like a shabby little weed fairy. Then she spots me and drops the snake to the sidewalk. It darts into a flower bed. She comes across the street and stops in front of our house.

She's looking up at the carved wood plaque that's shaped like a schooner and hangs by little brass chains from the porch eave. Daddy burned our name, *The Duprees*, into its bow with a soldering iron.

"The house with the ship," she says to me. Then she's pointing her finger at the house numbers above and saying each number out loud. Three. Two. Nine. "This is where Bailey lives," she says.

How does she know this? "You're a long way from home, Pearl Ann. Does your mama know where you are?"

She shrugs, then mumbles, "She don't care."

I can't help myself, and I ask her, "How do you know Bailey lives here?"

"Somebody said so." The lavender shadows beneath her pale eyes are beaded with perspiration. Threads of dirt circle her damp neck.

"You walked all the way over here by yourself?" She nods.

"You must be thirsty," I say. She nods again.

"And hungry?" This time, her eyes widen, and she says, "I reckon."

"Come on in," I say. "I'm hungry, too."

In the kitchen we eat baloney sandwiches washed down with lemonade. She's gobbling fast.

"How long have you known Bailey?" I ask.

She's eyeing the kitchen—Mama's spotless lino-leum, the apple green tablecloth with violets running all the way around the white borders, the calendar hanging next to the refrigerator with its picture of cocker spaniel puppies bunched up in a wicker basket.

"Them your puppies?" she asks.

"No, it's just a picture."

She studies the kitchen some more, then asks, "You live here all the time?"

This time I nod—and wait.

She's very solemn and hasn't smiled once. "He got me a ice-cream cone. Two times." She holds up her two index fingers. "Chocolate."

Is she asking me for another sandwich?

I get this sudden uneasy feeling that Bailey is listening to every word we're saying—maybe standing at the top of the stairs. I stand, pushing my chair back so quickly I startle Pearl Ann, and she raises her arm in front of her as though protecting herself. Her eyes are riveted to my face. Somehow I know better than to reassure her with a touch, so I say, "Let's go back out on the porch." I grab an orange from the fruit bowl on the counter and hand it to her. She holds it up to her nose and inhales deeply, then scoots off her chair and follows me through the house. She spies the picture of Francis in his soldier's uniform on the mantel and starts to say something, but I grab her grubby hand and lead her out to the porch.

"You want me to walk you back to town?"

She shakes her head no and says, "I seen Mr. Bonney over on Magnolla." I smile at the way she says Magnolia. "He lets me ride with him sometimes."

Sure enough, there's his car coming around the corner. Without a word, Pearl Ann runs for the beat-up old Packard as it slows down and pulls to the curb. Walter Bonney, the Sunshine Route Man, honks his horn when they pass by the house. Pearl Ann looks at me and waves without smiling. I think I hear someone behind me, but when I turn and reach for the screen door, no one's there.

WHO'S STANDING BEHIND ME?—
Thursday, July 10th

*I*t's only been this year, and especially since Bailey has shown up, that I've started wondering about who I am, you know, the big picture.

Deenie showed me her family's genealogy chart. It's in the form of a big tree, like a spreading oak, and there are these connecting names and dates written all over the thing. At first it was boring as Deenie droned on, pointing to this one and that one. But then she got to the very first Lady Aldina Mason back in the seventeenth century, who was only thirteen when she jumped from the church bell tower rather than marry some toad. The family swore it was an accident so that she could be buried in sanctified ground. Things haven't changed much. That's the way people still are, trying to protect their good names. In my mind I could see her, small and peaceful, laid out on a slab of stone with her hands folded in prayer like the pictures you see in history books.

Deenie told me that Lady Aldina was a Scorpio, too. "See," she said, trying to keep a straight face, "you Scorpios go to great lengths to prove a point."

All that day I thought about Lady Aldina and what her life might have been like. I ended up feeling envious of Deenie's road map to all the people she's a part of. A kind of homesickness actually set in, a kind of longing to know who are all of the people standing in back of me.

When you're growing up, you never give any thought to who your parents are. I mean, who they are as people, where they came from, that kind of thing. Growing up, they're just your mother and father, the ones who feed you and look after you and try to set you straight every inch of the way.

Daddy has rip-roaring tales of growing up in California, but mostly he likes to talk about how he went to San Francisco with an uncle when he was twelve, saw a mighty clipper sailing out of the bay, and from that day on, he says, he knew he was going to sea. Well, I guess that wasn't all peaches and cream, either, but he says that hard, treacherous life got into his blood.

From what I can tell, his folks are wild, tough people living by their wits all up and down the length of California. "Scattered from hell to breakfast," he says. Not a one of them has ever been here for a visit. When he's had a nip or two from the bottle he keeps locked in his bottom desk drawer, he tells about the first time he made port in Charleston and spied Barbara Munroe clerking at the drug store on the corner of King and Calhoun. "My treasure," he says, "my beautiful perfect girl." Mama says she never clerked in a drug store a day in her life, but her eyes sparkle.

She never talks about growing up, never talks about her people. When I got old enough to go to school and started wondering aloud where were my grandparents, my aunts and uncles, my cousins, she said most of them had died in a scarlet fever epidemic back long before I was born. "Are they angels like Charlotte?" I asked, but she didn't answer. All I know about Mama is that she grew up on a farm in Arkansas.

I remember once when Francis and I were little, a car pulled up in front of the house one day and sat there for a while. Mama finally went out to the curb and talked to the people in the car. Then they all came in—a man, a woman who looked like Mama, and two little tow-headed boys. I still remember their names, Arnie and Eddie. Those boys raised holy hell that weekend getting into everything, and Francis and I had the time of our lives.

Daddy was at sea, and Mama seemed sad and angry at the same time. I woke up in the middle of the night and heard Mama arguing with the woman down in the kitchen. It was kind of scary because Mama never raised her voice, and when they both started crying, I put my pillow over my head. The next day they left, and Francis and I ran like puppies after the car because we hated to see those little boys go. When I asked Mama once a few years later who they were, she said, "Nobody you need to worry your head about." Chances are good they were some of her kin.

I've been thinking and thinking, but I can't remember

one single time when I ever heard the name Bailey
mentioned.

CHARLOTTE'S ANGEL—*Monday, July 14th*

When Daddy's at sea, I sometimes wake up too early in the mornings from nervous dreams that fishtail out of sight the minute I open my eyes. I take comfort by slipping downstairs and curling up in his overstuffed chair by the front window. He's a big man, and over time the cushions have shaped themselves to him. When I sit there, it feels as if he's telling me that everything is all right. Sometimes I even open up his pipe rack on the magazine table and let the burnt, stale aroma from the pipe bowls drift into the air.

This morning as I pad through the archway into the living room, there sits Bailey in Daddy's chair. Anger slams through me so fast it almost knocks me off my feet. First Francis's room—now Daddy's chair. I want to race over and upend him out onto the floor, but the gray light of dawn filling up the room gives him a kind of spooky look, and instead, I take a step back and say, "Oh."

He has on his khaki pants but no shirt, and he's barefoot. His lean arms are surprisingly strong looking. There's that thick ropy scar across his chest. He nods, half smiles, and looks down at the porcelain figurine in his hands.

Charlotte's angel!

I walk over and pull it from his rough hands and set it back on the mantel. When I turn around, his head is cocked to one side, his eyes squinting more than usual, as if looking at me hurts. I flush. I know I'm being rude.

"Mama doesn't like anyone handling it," I say.

He nods, pursing his lips.

"It's Charlotte's," I explain as though he should know. When he just sits and says nothing, I spit it out again, "Charlotte!"

He makes a helpless gesture with his hands, then runs his fingers through his coarse blond hair, and I get flustered when I see the darker patches of hair in his armpits. It's too . . . animal-like. He lowers his arms and rests one hand on his chest.

"Where'd you get that scar?" I blurt out.

"Fighting for my life," he says softly.

"How?"

He ducks his head down and studies the scar. "Who's Charlotte?" he says and looks up at me.

"You mean Mama never told you?"

A melancholy look moves across his face like a shadow. "No, she never did."

I turn back to the mantel. The gold trim on the angel's wings is catching the first soft rays of morning sunlight.

"She's my sister. She died before I was born. Anyway . . . Mama says the angel is not to be disturbed."

"I reckon angels are always disturbed," he says, gazing out the window. "If you believe in things like angels."

This is the most he's ever said to me. My anger is slowly playing second fiddle to my growing curiosity. The room is quiet except for the mantel clock that's measuring my breath stroke for stroke. I wait for him to say something else. He doesn't.

"She only lived seven days," I say.

He leans forward, resting his elbows on his knees. I think maybe he's getting ready to stand up, and a spasm skitters through my stomach. Instead he squints up at me. "That's hardly enough time to get your feet wet," he says.

I don't like the way he says that; it sounds cold-hearted. Is he making some kind of joke? I always think I can see the truth in people's eyes if I look hard enough, but his face is closed—a mystery. Before I can say anything, he says, "She's probably still around here. Maybe up in that angel—you reckon?" He tilts his chin toward the figurine.

A rabbit runs over my grave—you know, those icy prickles that shiver down the back of your neck and spine. He has no way of knowing that when I was little, I'd sometimes wake up in the middle of the night hearing someone singing so softly it could have been the wind rustling through the magnolia leaves outside my window—and if I didn't open my eyes too wide and I lay very still, I could see a tiny girl, delicate as a silvery moth, sitting on the window seat. Once she even smiled at me.

My expression must be giving me away, because he says, "Nothing wrong with you, girl—you get that from the Munroes." He leans his head back against the chair and says, "I can tell you a story."

"O.K.," I say.

He sprawls his legs out in front of him and stares up at the ceiling. "When I was a young'un, there was a boarded-up root cellar at the edge of this cornfield. One day, just for the heck of it, I tried to pull off one of the boards, and this voice, hissing like a snake, came up outta there and told me to get away and leave him alone." He starts tapping his blunt fingertips against the chair arms. "I musta jumped six feet and tore off across that field to Granny Harper's house. She said it was just old Farmer Haddock's spirit hiding from a party of Cherokees traveling through, still too scared to come out after a hundred and fifty years."

He's looking at me steadily now, and I can't seem to look away. "If you got the sight," he says softly, "they come at you any way they can, slipping through the veil somehow."

Yes, slipping through the veil. I'm beginning to feel lightheaded, as if I could float right up to the ceiling. I hear myself say, "She doesn't let me see her anymore." He's saying something to me; I can see his lips moving, but I can't hear him. With a start, I realize I've said something that I want to take back! He looks like he might be getting ready to smile. Is he mocking me? I feel as if he's tricked me, as if I've stepped into something over my head. The air in the room seems warmer, heavier, and from somewhere up the street comes the familiar rattle of milk bottles as Tucker's dairy truck makes its morning rounds.

"I won't disturb that angel again," he says. Something in his expression reminds me of Francis. I almost trip over the footstool getting out of the room.

My heart is pounding hard and fast as I take the stairs two at a time. The minute I close my bedroom door behind me, I slump back against it and clench my eyes shut.

A little shadow flits across my mind. It's me. I'm so small—maybe four or five. I've dragged a chair from the kitchen to the mantel in the living room. I want to play with the gleaming angel that's been beckoning to me for as long as I can remember. Mama comes flying out of nowhere, slaps my hands, and sets me back down on the floor. "Don't ever touch that again!" she scolds. Then she's taking the chair back to the kitchen, but stops and glances over her shoulder. There's a look of pain on her face as she comes back and hugs me, trying to soothe my startled, hurt feelings.

She holds me on her lap and tells me about Charlotte, about how she was too beautiful for this world and how God missed her so much He sent an angel to bring her back to Him. I watch two tears roll down her cheeks. I ask her why God takes people back. She shakes her head as if she doesn't understand, either. Then she murmurs that life sometimes seems to be all about losing everyone you ever love.

For a long time after that, I often woke up in the mornings with this dread that one of them—Francis, Daddy, or Mama—had left with an angel during the night. But I don't think she ever realized how much she'd scared me. I think she was trying to tell me something altogether different. But what?

Last year I started noticing that sometimes a kind of wincing look crosses her face, a look I don't think she even knows is there. The day I finally asked her if she was sick, if something was wrong, she was in a bad mood and gave me a hard look. "Nothing for you to worry about," she snapped, and I backed off. Now, I'm beginning to wonder—what? I don't know—I think she's been in some kind of pain for a long, long time.

I'm wishing I hadn't gone downstairs this morning. I'm wishing I hadn't heard this man say that Charlotte's spirit might be inside some stupid figurine. Mama wouldn't want to hear anything like that; her Charlotte is in heaven playing around the throne of the Lord.

I hear him padding down the hallway, and I open my door as he's passing. "I hope you're not telling Mama stuff like that," I say, trying to sound concerned.

He pauses, his head drooping to one side as he looks down at me. "I didn't even know there was a Charlotte till you brought it up." His voice sounds different, with an edge to it.

"Well, Mama wouldn't like to hear anything like that. Only country people still believe all that stuff about ghosts. What I said about Charlotte . . ." His deepening scowl silences me, and I back away from him.

He doesn't say another word, just stalks on down to Francis's room and shuts the door behind him too hard.

Francis's room. Daddy's chair. Charlotte's angel. And just a little while ago, down in the living room, he lulled me into dropping my guard and reached inside my head easy as apple pie. That's scary. I better watch my step; he can't seem to make up his mind how he wants to act from one minute to the next. Yeah, I better watch it.

THE STALEMATE—*Thursday, July 17th*

*D*eenie and I bank our bikes like a couple of airplane aces, heading for the soft drink cooler at Reeves Gas Station. It's only ten-thirty, but the station at the edge of town is busier than usual—the sun already so hot and glary everybody's squinting. We drop our nickels into the cooler slot and grab a couple of Cokes from the slushy ice water inside. The first biting gulps leave us gasping and laughing. Deenie pulls a bag of potato chips off the wire rack next to the cooler and flips a nickel into the tin can on the top shelf. We flop on the yellowing grass under the oak tree shading the station. The smell of horse manure drifts softly on the lazy air; somewhere across the fields, somebody's stuck with cleaning out the barn this morning.

I've hardly munched two chips before Deenie says, "Look."

I'd recognize that gray, '39 Chevy coupe anywhere. John Howard Thompson steps out, sporting a fresh haircut—you know, all ears. He hurries around to the other side of the Chevy, opens the door, and out steps—a girl. I instantly know it's Jo Helen Graham. She's wearing a white piqué sundress, and her lipstick matches the little red hearts printed all over it. Her gleaming reddish brown hair is held back off her face with a thin red ribbon and cascades into flips and flirts around her shoulders. She has the tip of a lace-edged handkerchief tucked under her watchband—so Savannah. You can definitely tell she's seventeen.

"No boogers up that nose," says Deenie. My heart sinks.

John Howard doesn't see us; he's too busy strutting beside Jo Helen like they're headed out to their coronation. If pride is a sin, he's doomed. I hear him say, "Fill it up," to the oldest Reeves boy, Wayne. Ever since gas rationing was lifted last year, more and more people are tooling up their old cars and driving in to Charleston or Savannah on the weekends. It's only Thursday; I guess he's getting a head start.

Everybody, even Auntie Mason, agrees that John Howard and I were made for each other, but Daddy says no dating until I'm fifteen. Case closed. Jo Helen Graham could waltz away with the love of my life while I spend the next four months *accidentally* running into him every way I can dream up. Nobody told me she looked like this! All Arlene Hudson said was—*cute.*

They're heading for the cooler, and I pull back behind the tree.

"Don't worry," says Deenie. "You could be walking naked with your hair on fire, he wouldn't see you."

We flatten out in the grass and watch them. Jo Helen's handkerchief flutters down to the ground. So fast it's like a blur, Pearl Ann Wayland jumps from atop a pile of wood pallets behind the station and comes flying across the gravel. She stoops and snatches it up, sniffing toward it like some little critter. Then she balls it into a lacy bouquet, cups it to her nose, and inhales so deeply she begins to tilt backward.

"That thing is loaded with Savannah cologne, guaranteed," says Deenie.

Jo Helen holds out her hand to Pearl Ann and says, "Thank you, darlin'."

Pearl Ann frowns. Her lips twitch then stretch wide, showing raggedy edges of teeth. I half expect her to growl. She scrambles back atop the pallets, squats, and looks down at Jo Helen and John Howard, who've followed her. John Howard suddenly whirls around like he's been shot or something—his ears and neck are beet red.

Deenie snickers. "Pearl Ann probably doesn't have on any underwear."

When Jo Helen recovers from her surprise, she says, "Pull your dress down, darlin', and toss me my hanky."

"Yep," says Deenie and laughs out loud. John Howard hears her and turns toward us. His face is in a turmoil. He hasn't the vaguest idea of what to do next about Jo Helen Graham's lacy handkerchief. Deenie and I just lie in the grass staring back at him.

It's a stalemate. Pearl Ann has no intention of giving up the handkerchief without a fight. In frustration, Jo Helen's voice turns whiny. "I sure don't want to have to call the police. You don't want that, do you?"

Pearl Ann doesn't budge. Mr. Reeves comes around back, craning his neck like an old rooster trying to see what all the ruckus is about. He makes his way over to Pearl Ann and rattles the pallets. "What you doing up there, girl? Didn't I tell you to hightail it? Give this young lady her property."

Pearl Ann's squatting up there like a squirrel, taking a whiff of the handkerchief every so often. Jo Helen tries to catch John Howard's attention, but he's facing the other way, looking like he wishes the earth would open and receive him. She takes a couple of steps toward the pallets. "God really frowns on little girls who do this kind of thing," she says mournfully, as if she's actually concerned about Pearl Ann's soul now. "Wouldn't you like to show Him how sorry you are by giving me back my handkerchief?"

People are gathering round back, and Pearl Ann starts waving the handkerchief over her head. It swoops and flutters like an albino swift-tail swallow.

"Can't you put a stop to this?" Jo Helen is right up in Mr. Reeves's face, and he steps back, flustered. "Nasty little piece of trash," she says under her breath, but we all hear it.

Whatever she is—this sorry-looking child from the cheap, stale-beer side of town—it's not her fault. Jo Helen has just lost the popular vote.

Out of nowhere, there's Bailey. I bolt upright. He walks past everyone over to Pearl Ann. "I'll buy you two of those, and a whole lot prettier." His voice shocks me. It's loud and grating, like gravel in a bucket, not at all the way it sounds at home. He holds up his hand. He may be smiling; it's hard to tell.

She studies him. "Two?" she says finally. He nods. We're all watching her as she thinks it over, then she leans down and lays the handkerchief on the palm of his hand.

Jo Helen is relieved but clearly intimidated by tall, rough-looking Bailey, and her voice drops a good notch or two. "My grandmother gave that to me . . . it came all the way from England."

Deenie nudges me. "Are you as impressed as I am?" she says sarcastically.

Instead of giving her the handkerchief, Bailey walks over and drops it onto the rusty cooler lid. "In that case," he says, his voice harsh as razor nicks, "better wash this thing. No telling what the hell that girl's got."

Jo Helen's eyes flash. You can tell she's thinking *how dare this awful man talk to me like that.*

"For your information, I'm Mrs. Archie Graham's niece, and that handkerchief is practically an heirloom."

Bailey pretty much ignores her. He turns back to Pearl Ann and reaches up for her. Without hesitation, she leaps into his arms. He holds her close. Her chin is resting on his shoulder, and she watches us with steady eyes as they head on toward downtown.

Without a word between them, John Howard and Jo Helen get into the Chevy. She's sitting way over on her side glaring out the window, her mouth crimped to hold back angry tears. John Howard cuts his eyes over at her. I know that look; he's in way over his head.

Deenie says, "Did you notice how fat her ankles are?"

We bike on out to the skating rink to see who's hanging around. The inside of my stomach feels like a butterfly's in there having a ball. I giggle out loud. Sure glad I didn't miss all that!

SOMETHING'S NOT QUITE RIGHT—
Saturday, July 19th

*T*he doorbell rings, and Walter Bonney's lilting voice comes bubbling down the hallway. "Mrs. Dupree? Got some fine specials today!"

"Oh, Lord." Mama's eyes flick around the room as though she's looking for a place to hide. "Tell him . . . oh, tell him whatever, Afton."

Everyone in town likes Walter except Mama. Her only explanation is that he's too *familiar*. Auntie Mason laughs and says, "Of course, he's familiar, he's a route man." But Mama just does that little sniff with her nose. Her mind is made up.

He sells Mr. Sunshine products—hand lotion, kitchen brushes, laundry detergent, floor wax, wallpaper cleaner, mosquito repellent. You name it, Walter Bonney probably has a sample of it stuffed in his battered salesman's case. He's given Deenie and me lots of lifts from school when the weather's acting up, always with a silly joke to tell us and sometimes a free sample of what he calls girlie stuff, hand lotion or bath powder. I'm not fooled, though. I saw a kind of desperation in his eyes once, and I could never forget it.

He's hunched forward now, one hand cupped across his forehead, peering through the screen door. He's a paunchy, pink-faced little man with wisps of blond hair curling around the edges of his bald head. When he sees me coming down the hallway, he straightens up and breaks into a big sloppy smile.

"Morning, little lady! Sorry I missed you folks last time."

I smile quickly; last time we'd sat motionless in the living room, Mama especially grateful that the front door was closed. It took him forever to give up and leave.

"Mrs. Dupree got an order for me today?"

She doesn't, but his eyebrows are lifted with expectation. He has a habit of fingering the Purple Heart medal on his lapel when he asks for an order. Deenie calls it his incentive to buy.

"Put us down for a large-size hand lotion," I say. The heavy smell of too much aftershave doesn't quite cover his stale body odor, and I shift back a step.

He reaches into the inside pocket of his seersucker jacket and wrestles out his thick order pad and pencil.

"Just one?" A wheedling near laugh comes from the back of his throat like phlegm.

I pretend to be mulling it over, and we stand looking at each other until I break the spell, glancing past him at his dusty old Packard out front. It's so weighted down with boxes and bags in the backseat, it looks like an ailing critter barely able to drag its tail along. Pearl Ann Wayland's little head bobs up at the front passenger window. I look back at him just in time to catch an odd glint in his eyes, then he smiles.

"Second time this week I've picked her up out by Buford's Crossing."

"What's she doing way out there?"

He nods his head sadly. "She don't have nobody," he says.

"Her mama," I say.

"Yep." His voice is flat. He leans down and snaps the latches shut on his case. "So, that'll be it this week?" When I nod, he grips the worn leather handle and straightens up. The weight of the case gives him a lop-sided look as though one arm really is longer than the other. Then he does that thing I always wonder how long he practiced in the mirror, ducking his head to one side in a vaguely fawning way.

"Tell that pretty mama of yours that Walter Bonney extends his appreciation for her continued patronage."

"I sure will."

"Keep a song in your heart now!" he calls back over his shoulder before climbing into his old rattletrap. Pearl Ann waves at me as they pull away from the curb.

Back in the kitchen, I hurry to the sink and wash my hands. Mama is making sandwiches for lunch. "Tuna salad," she says. We eat quietly. Mama watches the clock. Her favorite Saturday morning radio program, *Alma and Her Singing Guitar*, comes on at 11:45.

"He had Pearl Ann Wayland in the car." When she doesn't answer, I add, "He said he keeps finding her out at Buford's Crossing."

Mama shakes her head and stirs her iced tea. She glances up at the kitchen clock again.

"Is Bailey going to be living with us for good?" It comes out of my mouth without warning.

The pulse in her throat is ticking a little faster, but she calmly finishes her sandwich before answering me. "No, he's not."

"How long is he going to be here?"

"Not all that long, Afton. Let's talk about it another time." She's not looking at me. "Clear off the table, would you? And rinse the dishes."

Before I can say another word, she's on her way to the living room and Alma's guitar. My cheeks are burning. Mama has politely told me once again to shut up and mind my own business. Why isn't this any of my business?

We've never been close. I don't know why. Francis could do no wrong in her eyes, but with me there's always been a distance that I can never get across. I sometimes wonder if it's because I don't have her blond look the way Francis did.

I envy the way Deenie and her mother enjoy being around each other. She told me last year when I was so angry with Mama about something I can't even remember now, that it was just unlucky star chemistry. She said Mama was a Pisces, overly sensitive and forever darting and hiding in the shallows at the far end of the pool. She said I was way too intense and prying for my Piscean mother. I wish I believed all this stuff—it might help.

All I know is that the older I get, the wider the distance between us grows, and now, with Bailey here, it has a sharper edge to it. They're so guarded when I'm around, shutting me out as though I'm a kid. Something's not quite right. What in the world could have happened to him in that prisoner of war camp that has to be kept such a big secret, anyway? Did he go crazy or something?

MY MIDDLE NAME IS CRESCENT—
Monday, July 21st

I dry the last glass and set it up in the cupboard; Mama hates for dishes to be left in the drain rack. She's in her sewing room keeping herself busy until *Mr. Keen, Tracer of Lost Persons* comes on. I've noticed this past year how she times whatever she's doing so she doesn't miss any of her radio programs—as if she'd rather be with them than with real people. She doesn't do this when Daddy's home.

Every once in a while I hear the metal racing of her treadle machine. It stops altogether, and the *Mr. Keen* music, "Someday I'll Find You," floats down the hallway toward me. Deenie says it's an old ricky-tick song from the thirties. I'd rather do most anything than listen to this program. Anyone over five can figure things out long before good old Mr. Keen patiently ties everything up in a nice bundle for his dumb assistant, Mike Clancy. Every time Mr. Keen explains the meaning of a clue that's obvious as a baseball bat, Mike says, "Saints preserve us, Mr. Keen!" Mama likes all these old-fashioned shows and hardly ever listens to programs like *Dragnet* or *Arthur Godfrey's Talent Scouts.*

Bailey disappeared out the back door right after supper with his usual "Thank you, Barbara." I peer through the kitchen window into the twilight outside, and there he is, sitting on the back steps. Well, this is a first. He seems to be at ease, not doing anything in particular, just sitting. Maybe I should go out and casually start up a conversation with him, make an extra effort for Mama's sake.

When I open the screen door and step out onto the porch, he turns toward me, and for an instant the face looking at me is so bleak, I want to turn right around and go back inside.

Instead, I tilt my chin skyward and say, "Would you look at the new little sliver of moon trying to make a showing." He frowns slightly. Some inner ticking cautions me to go slow. If there's one thing I've learned the past few weeks, it's how moody and changeable he is. Instead of walking over to the glider and sitting down, I lean against the doorframe, my hands tucked behind me.

He's looking at me but doesn't say anything. "I always feel good when there's a new moon. My middle name is Crescent. Daddy gave it to me because I was born under a waxing crescent moon." I pause, hoping he'll say something—anything. "Mama doesn't like it much." I give a little laugh. "She named me Afton. From that old Scottish folk song about the river Afton?" I hum a few bars.

He makes a clearing noise from deep in his throat. "She wanted my middle name to be Mary, like the girl in the song that's sleeping by the river." I laugh again. "But Daddy said he stood his ground because I was the first genuine moon maiden he ever knew." My words are stumbling on top of each other like dominoes going down.

"They're all pretty names," he mumbles and turns back around. The growing silence between us is broken by a rough sandpapery sound, and I realize that he is clasping and unclasping his big hands. But he isn't making a move to leave, so I keep going. Maybe I can somehow chip away a chunk or two of the wall between us.

"Daddy says that men who go to sea are tied to the stars," I say softly.

"Yeah?" His shoulders are hunched, and he seems to be pulling his head in closer to his body.

"Uh-huh, he showed both Francis and me how to find the Mariner's Star when we were little." When he doesn't answer, I say, "Polaris, the North Star. Daddy says it's the sailor's best friend because it's the one star that never moves, so if you know where it is in the sky, you can always navigate your way back to home port."

He murmurs something I can't quite make out.

"Soon as it gets a little darker, I can show you where it is right up there; you don't really need a compass. Everybody can find the Big Dipper, and then you just follow the Pointers right down to the end of the Little Dipper's handle." I walk over to the banister railing.

He doesn't move as I ramble on.

"Daddy says he wouldn't be a bit surprised if we all don't have a little piece of the North Star inside us . . . that navigates us in the right direction in times of trouble." I can feel the sudden tension in the air. Without meaning to, I've gone too far.

"That might not be true," he says, standing up.

"Well, Daddy's been all over the world. . . ." Right in the middle of my sentence, he steps down into the yard and crosses over to the driveway. Just that fast he's gone, leaving me with a mouthful of mush.

"Wait, I didn't mean anything . . . ," I call after him. What's wrong with him, anyway? I flop down on the old glider, and it creaks and shimmies more than usual, and a memory of Francis comes flooding in—the time he sneaked up behind me and gave me a surprise push too hard, and the glider tipped over. I wasn't hurt, but I screamed bloody murder, and Francis lit out for Auntie Mason's across the street.

I wonder what Francis would make of all this. Being a soldier himself, maybe he'd know what's wrong with Bailey. Something is so out of whack since he got here. Maybe I ought to mention to Daddy that he's here the next time I write. But Mama said, "Don't tell Daddy just yet." My head is beginning to throb. Maybe telling Daddy will cause something to happen that I don't expect. I sigh and look up at the silvery crescent moon hanging in the darkening purple sky. "So what do you think, Francis?" I whisper.

The screen door opens, and Mama says, "Who are you talking to, Afton?"

I was trying to talk with your nutty brother, Mama, but you know Bailey, why use two words when none will do. Of course, I don't say that. "Just thinking about Daddy," I murmur.

She lingers in the doorway, the light from the kitchen throwing a glow over her hair and shoulders. Sometimes I forget how pretty she is.

"Bailey go for his walk?" she asks, looking around the porch.

She didn't say *a* walk, she said *his* walk—so she *does* know that he's out prowling around all hours of the night.

I sigh and make a show of studying my fingernails; I might even be on the verge of shaking my head.

"And what is all that supposed to mean?" She tilts her head to one side with that slightly irritated expression she's been giving me the last couple of years. "You have to respect the privacy of others, Afton. Can't you just be nice? Before you know it, you and Bailey will be the best of friends."

"Mama," I say quietly, "I'll be fifteen in November."

But she doesn't get it. *"The Blue Grass Roundup*'s coming on," she says. The screen door slaps shut behind her as she heads back to the spotless old Crosley Console in the living room. I rock the glider back and forth slowly and think of Deenie at home listening to her Frank Sinatra records on her new RCA turntable.

LORDY LORD . . . WHITE FOLKS—
Wednesday, July 23rd

I'm sitting on the front steps drying my hair in the sun, waiting for Isaac to work his way around the corner of the house to the flower beds fronting each side of the porch. I need to ask him something. I hear the clatter of his gardening tools in his old wood bucket and his soft grunting as he crawls into sight.

"Hey, Isaac," I say. "Hot enough for you?"

He glances my way, then sits back on his haunches, pulls off his straw hat, and wipes the perspiration from his face and neck with the big handkerchief always trailing out of his overall bib pocket.

His thinning hair is cut real short again this summer, and the gray growing in it, especially all around the front, is showing soft and silvery against his brown scalp. The creases across his forehead and along either side of his mouth are deepening now, too, but the rest of his face is smooth and has a warm cast to it in the sunlight. He says that comes from his grandmother, who was a Florida Seminole.

"Why you sittin' out in this blazin' sun? Got to do with that old dog again?" He squints up at me. "If he still up under that bush, he ain't got you in the back of his head—'less you got a pan of food in hand." He does his little clucking sound under his breath.

"I'm drying my hair," I say, trying not to sound snippy. "And—and—I was trying to figure out how old you are."

"You must be runnin' out of things to think about."

"Gee, Isaac, I was just wondering, is all."

He grunts. "I been knowing you since day one, ain't I?"

That's as far as we're going to go with it. I try to think of how to sidle up to what I want to ask him without being too obvious; he knows me like a book.

"So, how your mama doin'?" I ask, falling into the rhythm of country talk the way I always do around him. "She back from Charleston?"

"Yeah, she back."

"Well, I know she glad to be back, too."

He cocks an eye at me. "What you want, Miss Afton?"

"I'm not wantin' nothing . . . just visiting a spell." I huff around, making a *tsking* sound. "No need for you to be so cranky."

"I ain't cranky," he mutters without looking at me. "It's muggy today." As far as he's concerned, that takes care of it. He leans forward on his knees, skimming his fingertips over the clumps of bright orange-yellow daisies. "Jus' look at them," he says, pride creeping into his voice.

"Yeah," I say, "they something, awright."

"Miss Jessup's flower garden been all ate up by some old renegade peacock out there." He shakes his head with a show of impatience. "He just come gobbling along whenever he please. All she want to do is cry about it. I tell her, 'less you want me to load up that shotgun, ain't nothing I can do about it."

"You shot him?"

"Not likely. She say he too pretty in his silly way to kill even if the devil is egging him on. We strung some chicken wire." He chuckles to himself. "Lot of good that gonna do—that old peacock think he own the whole road out there."

"He's a real peacock? With a great big tail fanning out?"

He decides to give me a look. "Ain't that what a peacock is."

"Well, I mean, where he come from?"

"Where do anything come from? They just show up, and that's that." Before I can say anything else, he says, "You so like Cap'n Charles." It's a little pin stick in my side, but I've got other fish to fry today.

When Bailey first showed up, I'd sometimes see him and Isaac pass a few words between them, but I notice lately that Bailey is steering clear of Isaac.

"Isaac," I say, "can I ask you something?"

"Here we go," he says, looking at me and shaking his head slightly from side to side. "I know that tone. Gettin' all proper and like so."

"I'm just wondering . . . did you and my uncle Bailey have words of some kind?"

Isaac pulls off his straw hat again and blots his face against his shirt sleeve. I can see he's weighing his thoughts, then he says, "I ain't messing around talking about nobody, Miss Afton." He plops his hat back on and pretends to be studying something in the flower bed.

"Well, I know something's wrong," I say. "I'm not a raw peanut anymore. I got eyes, Isaac. And I got a feeling in the pit of my stomach."

"I pity the poor boy marry you—he ain't gonna have no secrets." He's fussing at me now, and that means I'm edging close to irritating his sense of what's acceptable and what isn't. But he said that word—*secrets*—and I can't let it go.

"I can tell you got an opinion, Isaac, just by the way you acting."

Only the busy, muted sound of insects flitting around us intrudes upon a long, deep silence settling in. Then he says softly, "He ain't looking like nobody come back from no war."

I could swear a streak of pure electricity shoots through my head. I lean closer toward him. "What *does* he look like?"

He's steadily pulling up little weed sprouts and flicking them into the bucket next to him. "You ain't hearing this from me, you understand?" He glances up at me, waiting, and I nod.

"He got certain signs."

"Certain signs?" My heart does a funny, quick, double beat.

"What you call a ghost man—ain't nothing left to him no more."

A ghost man? I stare at the top of his straw hat, trying to figure out what that means. Isaac Cantrell knows more about people and why they're the way they are than anybody I know.

"What does that mean, Isaac?"

"It means I ain't said nothing, and I ain't sayin' no more." He pulls himself to his feet, slowly, biting his lower lip as if squelching pain. "Your hair look good and dry to me," he says. He stoops and picks up the bucket. "My work need to be gettin' done."

I've made him uncomfortable. I've known him all my life, and he feels like kin—but he's not. There's a dividing line, and he just told me to get back on my side of it.

"Want some lemonade?" I ask.

"Ice water'll do fine," he says. I can hear the relief in his voice. "Just put it on the table out back if you please."

As I head for the front screen door, I hear him mutter, "Lordy Lord . . . white folks."

A ghost man? Those words tumble, slip and slide around inside my mind. They ring so true—even though I don't know what they mean.

It's going on twelve-thirty. Mama's in the kitchen putting together a dinner plate for Isaac. She looks up when I walk in.

"You need to rub some Vaseline into the ends of your hair; you look like something wild," she says. Daddy would've said, "Glory be, look at that beautiful girl!"

She heaps the plate with black-eyed peas, dips into the pot for a ham hock, and then reaches into the bread cupboard for the half pan of yesterday's corn bread.

"I was hoping I could give some of that to—"

She cuts me off. "I'm not cooking for that old dog," she says without looking at me, but she leaves a small wedge in the pan after taking out most of it for Isaac's plate.

"Some of the peas, too?" I coax. She doesn't bother to answer me. "He kinda pretty, Mama, like a wolf or something out of a Jack London story."

"*He kinda pretty?* You've been out there talking to Isaac again, haven't you? You're getting too old to be talking that country talk, Afton." I know exactly what she's saying.

"Well, that old dog *is* pretty, Mama, in his way. I was thinking I'd name him Traveler. That sounds fitting for him, don't you think?"

"Name him!" She gives a look as if I've lost my mind.

"He almost licked my hand yesterday when I shoved the pan under the bush," I say.

"You better watch out that dog doesn't bite you, Afton. He could have anything—rabies—anything." She takes Isaac's plate out to the table on the back porch; he carries his own knife and spoon in his bib pocket. She comes back in, checks the clock. Time for one of her radio shows—probably good old *Ma Perkins*.

"Tell Isaac his dinner is ready." She motions toward the stove. "You can give that dog some peas, but don't use up all the pot liquor. . . ." She likes to use it in her okra soup. She sighs, then says, "Maybe you can get some potatoes going while you're at it." Potato salad for supper again tonight. Bailey's favorite. The ghost man's favorite. What in the world did Isaac mean?

I get his big tumbler off the pantry shelf, fill it with ice water, and set it out on the back porch table next to his dinner plate. I wish he were in a better mood today and I could ask him exactly what is a ghost man.

PUMPING CIRCLES—*Thursday, July 24th*

All I knew about Nona Wayland before Bailey showed up was that Pearl Ann was her kid and people said any old barn cat knew how to be a better mother. I'd never even seen her up close.

But that changed today when Deenie and I cut our bikes across the parking lot behind the Laughing Moon Bar and Grill. We wanted to hit Payson Road quicker and get out to the skating rink before John Howard and Jo Helen, the Savannah Bombshell, finished showing off. Word was they were out there acting like Fred Astaire and Ginger Rogers.

"Why do you want to torture yourself like this?" Deenie asks.

I can't even begin to answer her. There's a nail big as a railroad spike stuck in my heart. You'd think after the way Jo Helen Graham belittled Pearl Ann at Reeves Gas Station—all over a silly handkerchief—John Howard would have come to his senses.

"It's never gonna last," Deenie says. "She's probably got a boyfriend in Savannah."

"Maybe she's not going back to Savannah."

Deenie shrugs. "If it was me, I'd die before I'd go out there."

"Don't worry," I say, "I'm not gonna be all googly-eyed hanging over the railing staring, for God's sake. I just want to see how stupid they look."

"This is me you're talking to!" She throws me a smirk over her shoulder.

Before I can answer, the rear door of the Laughing Moon swings open, banging back against the building's lavender stucco wall. "Hey Good Lookin'," blaring from the jukebox, is streaming out the door along with Bailey and Nona Wayland. He has his arm around her waist, and they blink hard against the brilliant afternoon sun as they head for an old rustbucket pickup truck parked across the lot in the shade of a pecan tree.

"Another day, another dollar," she squeals.

I don't know why I do it, but I stand up on my bike pedals and slowly pump a circle around them.

"What're you doing here, Uncle Bailey? I thought you were out at the sawmill." When I start to circle again, he reaches out and grabs hold of the handlebars, stopping me cold. I jump down to keep from falling over.

"I guess you thought wrong," he says, leaning toward me. His breath reeks of beer and fried onions, and I turn my face away from him with a grimace. He adds, so softly I hardly hear, "Maybe it's my business what I do."

Nona Wayland squeals with laughter again. "I heard that! That's what I say, day in and day out, ain't nobody's business but my own!" Everything about her seems larger than life in a dingy, tacky way—her long henna-dyed hair coiling over her shoulders, her breasts and hips straining against her rumpled pink uniform, her smeary red mouth full of piano-key teeth.

"Come on, lover," she wheedles, grinning up at him. Her head's tilted so far back, you can see where her Pan-Cake makeup ends like a mask along her jaw line. Then she starts teasing him, nudging him toward the truck with her hip.

"You want me to tell Mama you might not be home for supper?" I give him a phony smile. He needs to know that I'm not a kid, that I know the score when I see it.

He doesn't miss a beat. "Does she know you're hanging around places like this?" He lets go of the handlebars with a little shove, sending me stumbling backward.

"Hey!" yells Deenie. "What'd you do that for?"

Ignoring us, they head for the truck and pile into the front seat. Nona Wayland, shrieking with laughter, slams her door over and over before it catches. The engine whines and growls like an old dog and finally sputters to life. As the truck roars out of the parking lot, Pearl Ann's tiny face appears like an apparition at the grimy back window.

"Did you see that, Deenie? There ought to be a law!"

"Against what?"

"You know what I mean! How long do you think she's been cooking in that truck?"

"Geez, Afton. Let it go, O.K.?" When I don't answer, she says, "Are we going out to the rink or not?"

"I can't stand him!" I cry. "He gives me the creeps. I wish he'd go back to wherever he came from!"

"If you go out to the rink all riled up like this, you'll regret it. Trust me."

I know she's right, so we head on down to Reeves for Cokes and chips and flop out under the big live oak.

Little by little, I give her chapter and verse—how Bailey prowls around town at night, how when he's home he mostly stays in Francis's bedroom pacing back and forth like something caged up, how whenever I try to talk to Mama about him I hit a brick wall, how even when I do try to be nice to him, he gets his back up as if I'm prying into his business.

"What business?" Deenie snorts. "Stacking lumber at the mill?"

"No. Before. I'm beginning to think he wasn't in the war. I think he's just out of some loony bin or something."

Her eyes narrow. "What makes you think that?"

"Something somebody said."

"Like what?"

"That he had certain signs . . . of a ghost man."

Deenie is staring at me with her mouth hanging open. For once I've left her speechless.

"I don't know what it means, either, but . . ."

Deenie looks off across the road, chewing on her lower lip. "Oh, my God!" She jerks upright.

"What?"

"Remember *Shadow of a Doubt* with Joseph Cotten and Teresa what's-her-name? You know, where her favorite uncle comes to visit, and she gradually finds out that he's not as nice as she thinks, that he actually goes around murdering rich old widows for their money?"

We stare at each other. Finally I say, "Rich old widows? You mean like Nona Wayland?"

She drains her bottle of Coke and sprawls back on the stubby, yellowing grass.

"Deenie," I say, "he couldn't charm warts off a frog. Sometimes I'd almost swear Mama's hiding him . . . doesn't want other people getting too close to him."

"Well, not really. She helped him get work at the sawmill, didn't she?"

"You know as well as I do, they'll hire anybody out there for day labor. They'd even hire Traveler if he knew how to haul and grunt."

"Traveler?"

"Yeah, that's what I named him. My dog."

"Your dog? Good Lord, Afton!"

"Look, Deenie, you're just not an animal lover, O.K.? Traveler needs me; before long I'll have him sleeping on the back porch."

She doesn't answer. She flattens out on her back and closes her eyes. I can tell by the smile playing at the corners of her mouth that she knows I'm looking at her.

After a while I ask, "What're you thinking?"

"I'm thinking how funny it is the way life over-takes people." She opens her eyes and smiles at me. "Deep, huh?" she says. "Straight from Gloria Starlight."

I'm impressed and repeat it in my mind, but I give Deenie a poke, saying, "Corny, with a capital C. Sounds just like the rest of Gloria Starlight's phony-baloney."

"Yeah," she says, "I knew you'd like it."

WHEN I GET HOME, there's a Baby Ruth candy bar on my dresser. I wonder if Mama is making a peace gesture, treating me as though I'm still a child she can pacify with a favorite candy bar. I shake my head—she doesn't understand how belittling of me that is. My stomach feels achy; when did I start finding so much fault with her?

After my bath, I go downstairs for supper. Bailey's nowhere in sight, but I don't ask about him. I don't care where he is or if he ever shows up again. Mama and I make small talk about the victory garden that we still keep going out in the backyard, but otherwise we eat in silence.

"You go listen to the radio, Mama. I'll wash the dishes," I say as she begins clearing the table.

She takes off her apron and folds it over her chair back.

"Bailey left a Baby Ruth up on your dresser," she says. "Did you see it?"

I know that Bailey hasn't been home. He's probably still with that Nona Wayland. I fake a smile, and she pats my arm and says, "He's trying as best he knows how to be your friend."

I watch her head toward the living room, and I don't know whether to laugh or cry.

GETTING TO KNOW JO HELEN—
Monday, July 28th

I pull open the screen door to Kirk's Dixie Mart, and there's Jo Helen Graham at the counter with a straw basket looped on one arm and holding a tiny shopping list up in front of her like a captured butterfly. I'm finally going to see her up close.

You never really get to know a person until you skirt around them awhile and watch how they act when you stick your uninvited nose into their business. For someone so small, Jo Helen has laid claim to the entire length of the counter by flouncing around unexpectedly. Old Mrs. Rusher, waiting her turn down at the end, has staked her claim with one hand firmly planted on a worn corner.

Jo Helen is wearing a yellow-and-blue sundress trimmed in white eyelet threaded with blue ribbon. Her hair is French braided down the back and tied with blue ribbon. Even her baby doll sandals are the same color blue. She looks like something out of a magazine. I've got on faded red pedal pushers, and one of my sandal straps popped as I walked into the store.

Mrs. Kirk is holding up a large can of Angel Flake Coconut. "This is all the flake we carry right now."

Jo Helen studies the can. "I don't know," she says. "That's a right good-sized can . . . isn't it? She definitely wrote one *small* can. See?" She holds the list out for Mrs. Kirk to take a look.

"Well, since this is the only size we ever carry, this is probably what she means." Mrs. Kirk ignores the list. She cocks her head to one side, sets the can on the counter, and inches it toward Jo Helen. Then she says, "I might have some small-size shredded in back."

Jo Helen looks around the store as if the answer is somewhere on one of the shelves. Then she says, "No, she wrote flaked. . . ."

I like Mrs. Kirk. She's plain as salt and just as dependable. She glances over at me.

"I need to get a couple cans of tuna and some peanut butter on account," I say. She nods and writes out a receipt for me. Then I lean over toward Jo Helen, pretending to study the can. "This isn't such a big can," I say.

Jo Helen turns to me. "You don't think so?"

I shake my head no.

"You'd get it?"

I nod my head yes.

While Jo Helen is busy looking at me, Mrs. Kirk pushes the can closer to her. "I'll just leave it here while you make up your mind." Her forced smile can't quite hide her cross expression as she heads up to the end of the counter to help Mrs. Rusher.

"My aunt is *so* particular and *so* penny wise . . . you can't imagine! But, you'd get the big can and hope it's O.K.?"

I smile and shrug helplessly. "My mother doesn't bake. . . ." Mama would faint if she heard me say this. One of her favorite solitary comforts is getting up in the middle of the night and baking cookies, sometimes even a pie or cake.

"She doesn't bake? At all?"

"Not much," I say. She's just standing there, looking at me with a little furrow between her eyebrows, so I say, "You're not from around here, are you?"

"Heavens, no!" She rolls her eyes. "It's so dinky," she says, "not at all like Savannah. I'm just visiting."

"Yeah, there's sure not much to do around here. You'll probably be glad to get back home."

I think I'm beginning to bore her—she's fiddling around with the coconut can and looking toward the front door. I notice for the first time that her nose is too pug. It'll probably get piggy in time.

"Well, back to the coconut flakes," I say.

She does a closeup inspection of me, actually evaluating my hair and face. "You look so familiar. Were you out at the church camp this week?" Before I can answer, *No, I watched you in action about two weeks ago out at Reeves Gas Station*, she says, "You could do a lot to help yourself. That's not your hairdo at all." She runs the tip of her tongue over her lower lip, studying me. "Why don't you fluff it out at the sides . . . maybe not so curly. . . ." She leans toward me and whispers in my ear, "You can buy little helpers now, you know. In any big department store."

"Helpers?"

She glances quickly at my shirt front.

I nod toward her full bosom. "Do you . . . you know?"

"Heavens, no!" She draws back, horrified. I've completely overstepped my bounds.

I try, too late, to strangle the laughter gurgling up out of my throat.

She looks over her shoulder to see if I'm laughing at something behind her.

"I just thought of a joke about—helpers," I say, "but I can't remember the punch line." Deenie would be proud of me.

"I know," she says. She knows? She's smiling at me with such concern. "I'm forever doing that . . . like which came first, the chicken or the silly hen." Her front teeth are crooked, one overlapping the other and streaked with lipstick. Suddenly, I'm feeling more lighthearted.

I glance at my watch. "For crying out loud," I say, "Mama's waiting on this tuna for lunch. I better get on back." I reach across her for one of the paper bags stacked on the counter, and she draws back as if I might soil her sundress.

"I've been working out in the garden," I say with a smile.

"It was sure nice seeing you again," she says. She doesn't have the vaguest idea who I am. She picks up the can of Angel Flake Coconut and turns it round and round in her dainty hands, reading the label and sighing.

"If I go ahead and get this," she says to Mrs. Kirk, "and Aunt Harriet throws a fit, can I return it?"

Mrs. Kirk looks up, plainly sick to death of Jo Helen's coconut dilemma. "By all means," she murmurs and goes back to toting up Mrs. Rusher's bill.

I get the cans of tuna and the peanut butter off the shelves, drop them in the bag, and head toward the front of the store.

When I push open the screen door, I run right into John Howard. He smells so good, and the sun dancing on his brick-red hair dazzles my eyes. "Afton!" he says, and his face lights up like he just bit into a Hershey bar. My heart kicks me in the chest. "Where you been keeping yourself?" he says. I give him a quick, friendly, "Hey, John Howard," as I brush past him. I know he's watching me walk my bicycle up the street—Jo Helen is beginning to wear thin.

THE CLOSET OF SORROWS—
Thursday, July 31st

I drift lazily to the top of my dream. Francis and I have been sitting on the back steps tossing smooth, white pebbles into a bucket about three feet out in the yard. It's a game with no rules, and my pebbles keep hitting the rim of the bucket and popping off to the ground. Francis puts his arm around me and says, "A miss is as good as a mile." I nod as if I understand. He checks his watch. "Gotta go," he says and rises slowly up into the sky.

I wake to a perfect summer morning. The lush, sweet scent from the magnolia tree out front drifts in on a soft breeze. I roll over on my stomach and watch the thin voile curtains ripple, lift from the screen, and fall back. Francis has left a vacant place in the very air around me.

A family of mockingbirds lives up in the crown of the magnolia. They're squabbling, fluttering and flapping down through the branches, each looking to get dibs on the coolest, darkest perch. I used to wonder how they knew to do that. Francis said once that it was all instinct, that they're born knowing how to do these things. I didn't quite get it. Instinct. What happens when one of them dies? What does their instinct tell them then? I feel such an ache, a longing to see Francis. All those people who told me it would get better with time lied. It doesn't get better at all—I just learned to keep it to myself.

I sit up on the side of the bed. I need to touch something that belonged to him. I need to reassure myself that he ran up and down these stairs—that he carried me, screaming with skinned knees and a broken wrist, all the way home from the skating rink. Maybe I can slip my hand inside his baseball glove and somehow reach back across time.

THE HOUSE IS QUIET. Bailey is at the sawmill. Mama has left a note on the kitchen table saying she's across the street helping Auntie Mason put up her peach preserves. Folks around here live in hope of getting their hands on a jar of Auntie Mason's famous peach preserves.

I walk by the closet under the stairway two or three times, not sure I want to open the door. Mama's worst sorrows sit inside that small dark space. Charlotte's frilly little bassinet is pushed to the back. I heard Mama once say that she hadn't been able to put her new baby—that would be me—into the little bed her first daughter died in, and yet she hadn't been able to part with the bassinet, either. All of Francis's boy stuff—games, comic books, even his first fishing rod—are shut away out of sight in there, too.

I watch my hand reach for the doorknob and slowly
turn it. The door creaks as it swings open. The baseball
mitt is hanging on a hook on the back of the door. I
trace my fingers over its worn lacings, then lift it off
the hook and cup it to my face and inhale the fusty
smell of my brother's sweat. I don't cry anymore; the
missing goes layers deeper than that now. Francis
Dupree won't be coming back this way. Ever.

It's funny how fate, or whatever you want to call it,
taps you on the shoulder and whispers in your ear. I hang
Francis's mitt back on its hook and start to close the door.
Instead, some impulse makes me reach inside the closet
and pull on the light cord.

The first thing that catches my eye is Mama's big,
old Christmas cookie tin up at the end of the top shelf.
I know it by heart from all the years it sat on the lace
doily atop her dresser. It's painted in soft greens and
reds and trimmed in gold. The Currier and Ives skaters
on the lid glide serenely across a pond set amid snow-
banks and fir trees. It's full of report cards, crayon
drawings, school essays. I'm pretty sure that on top of
it all lies the telegram telling us that Francis Dupree's
life is over and done with.

I stretch up, reaching, tipping the tin down toward
me, then I duck as it leaps into the air, its lid flying off
and papers sailing everywhere. When I open my eyes,
the tin is lying upside down in Charlotte's bassinet. I
turn it over. A false bottom of gold-colored cardboard
has been knocked loose. There's an envelope glued to
the underside. If this is something I'm supposed to see,

it wouldn't be hidden like this. I can't help myself; I work the envelope loose and pull up the flap.

The photographs are faded; one is of three young girls in old-timey clothes—pinafores and black boots. You can tell they're sisters. There's something familiar about the expression of the small one in the middle— I'm sure it's Mama. That same small girl is in the other photograph also, standing shoulder to shoulder next to a little boy. They're holding hands, just barely smiling. I turn it over. The faded ink reads *Bailey & Barbara 10 yrs old, Mar 14, 1917.* For a minute I get so lightheaded I can't breathe. My hand shakes like crazy as I hold the photograph up to the light, trying to get a better look. I'm having a hard time getting this through my head. I turn the picture over and read the inscription again and again. Bailey is Mama's *twin?*

I think I hear someone coming up the front walkway, and I rush with pounding heart to put everything back into the box, jamming the lid down tightly, and shoving it up onto the shelf. My mind is galloping a mile a minute as I pull the light cord and close the closet door. There are more than sorrows sitting inside that dark space—there are secrets. Mama's secrets.

August 1947

Sun in Scorpio

Eventually you will challenge the meaning of your life and strive unflinchingly to find its deeper purpose. Your keyword is: Regeneration.

Moon in Aquarius

It's likely that you'll make some painful mistakes in dealing with others early on, but in time you'll learn to balance the constant struggle between your demanding intellect and your often unpredictable emotions.

Scorpio Rising

At some point in your life you will undergo a major inner transformation, deeply affecting the way in which your ego expresses itself.

THE SIDE TRIP—*Monday, August 4th*

The heat inside the old bus bumping along to town is stifling. The windows are wide open, but there's not even a hint of cross breeze. Every once in a while, a fly tracking overhead gives up and drops like a withered raisin. Strings of sweat are sliding down my neck and arms, and the backs of my thighs are squishing around on the old, cracked leather seat. It's almost too much of an effort to breathe, and my calf muscles are starting to cramp up. I'm thinking I should get off and find some shade for a little while; it's not that long a walk home.

The only other people left on the bus are Jackson Smith, the driver, and Jennie Cook, who has a crush on him. She didn't volunteer to help rake and weed the cemetery out of any respect for the Departed like the rest of us. She spent most of her time dawdling all moony-eyed around Jackson, making him jumpier than a grasshopper.

When we turn onto Dexter Road and I tell Jackson I want off, he shoots me a pleading look. I try to say something funny, but it's too much of an effort. I hop down, make a feeble show of kicking out my leg muscles, and watch the old rolling oven rattle on down the road. It's at least five degrees cooler outside.

Without much thought, I head out across Carlan's Pasture for the creek. Nobody comes out here to Hingle Creek anymore. After old man Carlan built his spite dam to get even with the Lesters, the creek dried up to little more than a mudhole, and in the summer it's just a bleached-out, dry-as-bone bed littered with rocks and rusted-out cans and broken bottles. The pathway is still here but steadily overgrowing with cockleburs. I step gingerly so I don't suddenly come up on a snake.

The farther I follow the path in among the pines, the quieter it gets as the air thickens with the musty smell of old moss. The thatchy grass is pushing its way through a carpet of dried pine needles that crackles softly under my sandals. Even the wildflowers are drooping. Birds, mute and drowsy, perch in whatever shade they can find on the branches of scrubby pines and don't seem to notice or care that I'm here. I stop and look around, and a loneliness drifts over me.

I reach up and finger the gold locket hanging around my sweaty neck. I snap it open as if the picture of Francis inside can look out and remember, too, how we raced along this path just a few years ago. I haven't been out here since Francis was drafted. It seems so . . . abandoned.

I want to let my brother go. I want to say, *Good-bye, Francis. I'll love you forever.* But I haven't been able to do it yet. Maybe it comes from all those years that I tagged along behind him every chance I got, and he'd try to shoo me on back to the house, but I was like some little bulldog. Finally he'd have to promise me a ride on the handlebars of his bike, maybe all the way out to the skating rink, if I'd just stop tracking after him. When I think of stuff like that, a flood latch inside trips, and I almost drown in my longing to see him just one more time.

I look at my watch. Five-thirty. The hottest part of the day. My underwear is sticking to me like a second skin, and I'm getting so thirsty my tongue is sticking to the roof of my mouth. Maybe this isn't such a good idea after all. I should have toughed it out on the bus and gone home. Mama's probably steeping the tea for supper right now. Potato salad and cold ham washed down with amber, sweet, lemony tea loaded with chipped ice.

But he'll be there, too—Bailey—probably sitting out on the back porch glider, with his restless hands, shifting his feet on the smooth boards. In no time at all, he's filled the house with this feeling that something is hovering just out of sight. The other day I felt the hairs go up on the back of my neck as I walked down the hallway, and he wasn't even home. Sometimes he looks as if he might smile at you, might actually open his mouth and start a conversation. Other times he's scowling, ducking his head, hiding out in Francis's room. He unnerves me. Yes, that's it exactly. He unnerves me. Is that really why I got off the bus? To keep from going home? I hate that thought.

I almost jump out of my skin as a shocking sound hurtles toward me—the cries of something or someone in pain. My first instinct is to get out of here fast, but I'm rooted to the spot. Slowly my curiosity moves me toward the sound. Maybe someone's hurt. Maybe the good Lord put me right here, right now, to help someone. The sound is ebbing, and the closer I come to it, the more it laps back into the pain it came from. The creek is just ahead. I slip up behind the trunk of the old live oak.

There's a man sprawled facedown on the dried-out creek bank, his shoulders hunched and shuddering as he hollers gibberish into the ground. His voice is hoarse and pleading. He begins beating the ground with his fists and then pulls himself to his knees and crawls around on all fours like some blind creature spit up out of the earth. It's Bailey!

I am standing so rigid my calf muscles finally seize up, and my breathing seems to have stopped altogether.

He rears up like an animal trying to break loose from its chain, then falls back onto the ground sobbing, his arms wrapped over his head as if protecting himself. And I hear, plain as day, the name . . . over and over . . . *Susan*. Finally he's quiet, but the sound of my racing blood is thundering in my ears.

I squeeze my eyelids tight—I don't want to see this—but the darkness of trying to shut it out is even worse. I have to get out of here. I have to not be in this place. I ease back, and the pine needles crackle. He lifts his head. I know he can't see me, but I feel his eyes zeroing in on me, and I throw all caution away and wheel around to run. My foot catches in a snarl of underbrush, and I go down. I'm thrashing around, trying to pull free. Then I'm up, and only as I tear back across Carlan's Pasture and head for Dexter Road do I realize that I'm whimpering, my mind blistered with fear.

I'm running hard as I career out onto the road. I hear something coming up behind me. Walter Bonney's old Packard appears alongside like a ghost out of the pines. His pink, blurry face is leaning toward me out the window.

"What's wrong?" he hollers.

I stumble on, my breath stacking up in my throat. I hear the car door slam and then footsteps behind me. I twist my head around, and all I can think is how piggy Walter Bonney looks, jiggling and puffing down the road after me. Then he's close enough to reach out and grab my arm.

"Afton," he hollers, "stop! It's me, Walter Bonney. Get in the car." I try to pull away from him, but he hangs on. "Come on," he says, "it's O.K. It's O.K. I'll take you home."

Inside, the old Packard is a worse oven than the bus; the nauseating smells of lotions and cleaners and cheap perfumes are laced with a faint mildew odor rising from the threadbare upholstery. I glance toward the backseat, half expecting to see Pearl Ann's head pop up from somewhere among the jumble of dog-eared boxes and bags. I'm awash in my own sweat. I stink; I smell my own fear, and I lean toward the open window, gasping for air.

He doesn't say anything as we drive toward town, but out of the corner of my eye, I see him looking at me

every once in a while. Finally he says, "Some boy giving
you trouble?"

I shake my head no.

"Well, I'm sure not going to say nothin' to anybody.
If that was the case."

"No," I say, "I just got scared."

"Yeah?"

My mind is racing to build him a believable story.
"Might have been a wild pig," I say.

He grunts softly. "Nobody comes out this way
much," he says. It's really a question. He waits to see
what I'll say.

"I was going to gather some of those little pine
cones for . . . you know, crafts out at the church camp."

"Hey, now that's a good idea," he bursts in. "I was
thinkin' along those lines awhile back . . . they're just
sittin' there, free as all get-out . . . you could dab a little
gold paint here and there . . . make 'em up into Christmas
decorations . . . some green and red ribbons and . . ."

My pounding heart begins to settle down. I'm glad
he's talking and that I don't have to think. We pass
Magnolia Street, then Wisteria, then turn onto Lilac. I
take a deep breath, and suddenly, like a rock smashing
into the dusty windshield, the image of Bailey crawling
around explodes inside my head, and I'm shaking again.
We pull up in front of my house, and I reach for the
door handle.

"You sure you're O.K.?"

"Thanks, Mr. Bonney," I say as I get out.

"Don't worry. Mum's the word." He smiles as though we now have this big secret.

I run on faltering legs up across the porch and into the house and stumble up the stairs. I lock my bedroom door behind me and dive for my bed.

Mama calls up the stairs after me, "Is that you, Afton?"

"Yes," I yell. I'm trembling from head to foot. Now I know what's wrong. Bailey Munroe is all messed up—crazy.

Reaching for Polaris—
Thursday, August 7th

I've started three letters to Daddy this morning only to ball them up. How do I say what I need to say?

> *Dear Daddy,*
>
> *There's a man staying in our house who's probably crazy.*
>
> *He's Mama's brother, and his name is Bailey Munroe. Do you know about him? Has she ever said anything about him to you? Mrs. Hudson has blabbed all over town that he's a war veteran and has been in the hospital for a long time. I don't think so, Daddy. I have this feeling that they're hiding something. I stay as far away from him as possible. When I was at the* Herald *with Deenie the other day, Mr. Mason was working on an article about veterans in the area and asked me what military outfit my uncle Bailey served in. I don't know that, Daddy. Then he asked me if he got wounded in the war.*

There's a big scar on his chest, so yes, I guess he did, that's what I told Mr. Mason. But I don't know if I really believe that.

Now, how in the world can I send a letter like that to Daddy? I ball it up and flip it across the room with the others. Maybe I ought to go downstairs and tell Mama what I saw out at Hingle Creek. Maybe I ought to tell her that I know Bailey's nuttier than a dingbat and that sooner or later . . . what?

There's a tap on my door, and Mama is saying, "I brought up the new *Ladies' Home Journal* for you, Afton."

I turn the key in the lock and pull the door open.

"Why in the world is your door locked?"

I feel a flush spread up from my neck and sting my cheeks. She comes into the room. "Maybe this'll help perk up your spirits." She lays the magazine on the dresser. She floors me sometimes, the way she skirts around things. She knows there's a lot more tension in the house lately, but she'll do everything except take a look at it.

I reach out and touch her arm. She turns, expectant. The delicate shadows beneath her eyes are deeper than I remember.

"Mama," I hear the nervous quaver in my voice, "there's something wrong with him. . . ."

She actually puts her fingertips to my mouth and shushes me. "Please don't, Afton." Then she slips right back into let's pretend. "Why don't you go through the *Journal*?"

Before I can collect myself and say a word, she moves toward the door, scanning the room as she goes. She frowns when she sees the paper wads by the window.

"Isn't that your new stationery?"

I lift my chin a little defiantly. "I'm trying to write to Daddy."

"Afton," she says, her voice sliding into muted disapproval. I wait, and she smiles wearily.

"You're not as grown as you think. A lot of terrible things happen in this world. Can't you trust me to do what I know in my heart is best right now?" When I don't answer, she says, "Bailey will be gone before you know it, and then we'll sit down and have a long talk, and you'll be glad, more than glad, then that you were a little more thoughtful toward him."

"Why can't we talk now?" I blurt out. I'm on the verge of telling her I found the hidden photographs in the closet.

But, as she's studying my face, I see the softness go out of her own, and my neck stiffens.

"You haven't heard a word I said, have you?" She sighs deeply. "I didn't know Bailey was going to show up, Afton. It was as much a surprise to me as it was to you. Please don't interfere and write to Charles about this," she says. "And please, don't be making such a big show of locking your door. Whatever you may think of him, he has feelings. We can hear it clicking all over the house."

We? She said *we.* I feel as though she's chosen up sides, and I'm the loser. A streak of red flares up behind my eyes.

"There's something wrong with him! You *know* there's something wrong with him!" I can't believe I've raised my voice to her. From the look on her face, I might as well have slapped her. I step back. "I'm afraid of him," I whisper.

"He wouldn't harm a hair on your head." Her voice has turned defensive. "He'll be gone soon enough. Until then, by all means, lock your door, Afton, and while you're at it, lock your heart up, too!" She closes the door behind her with a quick, firm stroke.

I'm stunned. Somewhere in the back of my mind, I hear Deenie explaining to me why the Baker twins in the grade just ahead of us live in a world of their own. *Anybody who thinks they can come between those two has another think coming!* Those were her exact words. Well, just great, Bailey and Barbara . . . Barbara and Bailey! As if in retaliation, I stalk to the door and turn the key in the lock. It feels like having the last word. I throw myself across the bed and lie staring up at the ceiling, but no answers appear. I reach my hand up between my breasts and press in hard, searching for the beat of my heart. "Polaris," I whisper, "where are you?"

SOMEWHERE AWAY FROM DANGER—
Saturday, August 9th

The dog is gone. Traveler—he's been gone for two days now. Thursday night I watched from my bedroom window as Bailey paused at the end of the front walkway and slapped his thigh, but the dog didn't come out of the bushes. Bailey waited for a couple of minutes, then shoved his hands into his pants pockets and went on up the street without so much as a backward glance.

In the morning I took out a pan of scraps, but the dog wasn't there. Isaac shook his head and said I shouldn't have named him, that it put too heavy a burden on the old dog. I said I just wanted the dog to know that he finally belonged to someone. Isaac said that wasn't how the dog saw it. He said the dog probably figured out that I was trying to get him to be something he couldn't be. I didn't want to hear all that, and I walked all up and down Lilac, Wisteria, and Magnolia calling, "Here, Traveler."

When I got back, Isaac said, "That dog don't know Traveler from a hole in the ground. You want a dog gonna be your own, that one ain't it." I went to bed last night with a little prayer that Traveler might decide to come on back.

But the dog's not there again this morning. Auntie Mason must've been talking to Isaac, because she comes across the street while I'm checking under the bushes and says the worst thing I could've done to myself is name the dog—that most old road dogs don't trust people enough to let down their guard. I open my mouth to dispute that, but she steps right in and says, "Afton, that old dog only stayed for the food." I've been feeding him good. I even bought him a soupbone with my own money—one of those big, juicy ham knuckles like Mama uses in her okra soup. Why did he just up and leave?

Deenie calls—do I want to go out to the skating rink later? There's going to be a twenty-lap showdown between Billy Tisdale and some hotshot from Charleston. But all I can think of is that dog. I tell her he's gone.

"Well, you did name him Traveler." She laughs like it's a big joke.

"It's not funny," I say.

"Aw gee, Afton, it's just your lucky day!"

That really puts a knot in my hair. "He's old and helpless," I tell her. "He needs somebody to at least feed him."

"Evidently he didn't think so."

"Maybe something scared him off."

"Yeah, well, he really was pretty stinky. You could smell him half a block away." Then she says the oddest thing. "Maybe we're going to have an earthquake or something."

"What?"

She's hooked me again—and patiently explains that *Astrology for the Millions,* her favorite magazine, says animals sense stuff like that. Birds, cats, the whole kit and caboodle—they know it's coming.

"Deenie, I'm not in the mood for all that gobbledegook."

"It's not gobbledegook! Their senses are about a thousand times better than ours! I can show you in the magazine."

You'll never win an argument with Deenie about this stuff. She has all the answers and can come up with new ones at the drop of a hat. While she's rattling on, I'm wondering—can they hear creaking, groaning deep down inside the earth? And so then, they what? Pick up and leave?

"Where would he go?" I ask her.

"Somewhere away from danger," she says.

"But where?"

She flips. "Good God, Afton, I don't know! It's a theory! You know, t-h-e-o-r-y!" Then she says, "I have to go. Daddy wants me down at the paper this morning to help send out subscription notices." Before she hangs up, she heaves a big sigh. "It's just a beat-up old dog, Afton. You're so relentless sometimes, it drives me crazy!"

"Relentless?"

"Scorpio to the core—and then some," she says.

I don't answer, and she says, "You really need to be at the rink this afternoon to root for Billy, O.K.? Come on by the *Herald* around one-thirty. I should be done by then, but hey—I don't want to spend all afternoon talking about a ratty old dog, O.K.?"

THE HOTSHOT FROM CHARLESTON, some guy named Doug Farrell, wins the race, but Billy's happy—he finally gets a date with his dream girl, Clarisse Kirk.

The dog is still gone when I get home.

Mama, coming out on the front porch with Auntie Mason, says, "Why're you trotting back and forth to that bush? You're getting too old for this nonsense. Can't you see he's gone?"

Auntie Mason nods in agreement and says, "That old boy just moved along. They wander around, hither and yon. Maybe he'll turn up again if he gets good and hungry."

Later Mama calls me in for supper. I'm not hungry. I sit out on the front porch steps most of the evening waiting, but he never shows up.

As soon as Bailey comes shambling from around back and heads for the street, I go inside. Mama's in the living room listening to the *Grand Ole Opry*. She left a ham-salad sandwich on the table for me. As the deep, growling voice of Ernest Tubb, the Texas Troubadour, fills up the hallway, I pour a glass of lemonade to wash the sandwich down. "I'm walking the floor over you," he sings, and my throat tightens and I have a hard time swallowing. I can't believe how much I'm missing that old dog.

CAUGHT OFF GUARD—*Monday, August 11th*

*I*t's six-thirty, and the late afternoon sun is glowing like melted gold through the trees. The bus is almost empty as I get off at Lilac and Beaumont. I walk the half block home, and as I start up the porch steps, I see him at the far end in the luminous shade thrown by the big magnolia. He's sitting on the porch floor, smoking a cigarette, his back resting against the house, his knees drawn up. I hesitate and start to back down the steps, but he says, "Wait."

I stop and look at him. My scalp is tingling.

"Someone stopped by . . . looking for you."

"What'd she want?"

"A guy in a . . ."

My heart jumps. John Howard! ". . . gray Chevy coupe?"

"Yeah."

I step down, and before I can move away, he says again, "Wait."

My stomach does a flip-flop, and I'm ready to run if I have to.

He stands and walks slowly toward me. I'm breathing funny, jumpy and erratic. He stops about two feet away, leans against the porch banister, and takes a deep draw on the cigarette he's already smoked down to his knuckles. He flicks the stub out into the yard.

"You scared of me?" He has Mama's way of not looking directly at you at times. Right now, his eyes are just off kilter enough to rattle me. His question is unexpected, even painful, taking me off guard.

"I can tell," he says. "Reckon I don't blame you."

Part of me wants to deny it, and part of me is feeling trapped. All of me wants to get away from him, and fast.

"I don't know where you got that idea," I say quietly.

"Barbara. She says you're scared of me." He studies his boots. "She says I have to try to do better than this."

I'm pretty sure he's either outright crazy or unstrung from something, and I don't want to say the wrong thing. I try to inch away from him.

"I've forgotten how . . . ," he says. "I don't know how . . . to be . . . anymore." His voice is creaking, like a rusty hinge trying to open. I stand still. Is he going to tell me something?

"That was you out there the other day, wasn't it?"

"What?"

"Didn't mean nothing . . . just things all bollixed up inside."

Itchy trickles of perspiration slide down from my armpits.

"I found this behind that oak tree after you left."

He reaches into his shirt pocket, then holds out his hand. My gold locket winks in the fading sun. My initials are engraved on the front of it, and I'm sure he opened it and saw the picture of Francis.

"I couldn't find the chain," he said.

I'm floundering, my face hot with embarrassment. I reach up and snatch it. There's a look on his face that I've only seen once before—when Francis found the little squirrel in the backyard. It didn't have a mark on it, but as we stooped down to look at it, the light went out of its eyes.

"I'll be gone before long," he says. "Just . . . just don't . . ." He straightens up, moving away from the porch banister, and I draw back instantly. He walks down the steps past me, smelling of sawdust and sweat. "I shouldn't have come here," he mumbles to himself.

I watch him head on out Lilac, his hands shoved into his pockets, his head gradually settling down into his shoulders.

Mama's in the doorway. "Where'd Bailey go?" she asks, wiping her hands on her apron. "Supper's almost ready."

"Went on up the street," I say evenly and breathe a sigh of relief that I can eat supper tonight without him at the table.

"Did you two have a chance to talk?" She's squinting her eyes against the setting sun, and for an instant she looks blind. I suddenly want to shake her and tell her how I saw him crawling around out at Hingle Creek. Instead, I tell her that he said John Howard stopped by looking for me.

"See," Mama says, "I told you it was just a phase."

Over our fried chicken and biscuits she tells me what Lamont Cranston, The Shadow, was up to last night. She talks about these people as if they're real, as if they could walk into the room at any minute, sit down, and have supper with us. On an impulse I don't understand, I reach over and kiss her on the cheek. She stops in midsentence and blinks back her emotion.

"You're a good girl, Afton. I knew you'd do the right thing."

I have no idea what she's talking about. I don't like Bailey. I will never like Bailey. I'm afraid of Bailey.

But she seems to relax, leaning back and sipping her iced tea. "Things are going to work out just fine," she says. "There's a minister in Charleston who helps men like Bailey get on their feet. I heard back from him this morning." She pats the envelope in her apron pocket.

"What'd he say?" I'm not moving a hair.

"He said he'll be coming out this way right after Labor Day and . . ." She stops and sets her glass down. I could almost swear something in the kitchen shifts. "If I could just know that Bailey is safe and sound in Charleston with someone who understands what he's been through and will help him . . . and I could see him once in a while . . ."

I barely whisper the question. "Exactly what has he been through, Mama?"

Her fingertips trace around the embroidered violets on the tablecloth, then she pats my hand. "It's not that I don't trust you, Afton," she says finally. "It's other people. I'm just trying to protect you . . . from other people. We'll talk when he's gone, I promise." I know in my heart she won't tell me the whole truth, only what suits her.

A prickly thought flits through my mind that she's protecting *herself*. I become surer of this when she says with a slight smile, "Things are going to work out all right, you'll see, and we'll just keep it all to ourselves." She glances at the kitchen clock. Time for *Carolina Hoedown*.

Later, up in my room behind the locked door, I desperately try to figure out what she was talking about, but the missing puzzle piece is too big. I know now that she's connected to Bailey as only twins are; it's in her eyes, it's in every gesture she makes toward him. But something is running just beneath the surface and taking its toll on her—and it's been going on a long time.

A STUPID DEATH—*Wednesday, August 13th*

I almost miss the item on page three of the *Herald* this morning. It sure isn't screaming for attention. It's tucked down at the bottom of column four.

Woman Found Dead

A local waitress, Nona Wayland, 28, employed at the Laughing Moon Bar and Grill, was found dead at approximately 3:30 this morning at the foot of the outside stairway leading up to her rooms at 32-B Courtland Street. Preliminary medical examination revealed that she was intoxicated at the time of her death, which is being attributed to a broken neck sustained in the fall down the stairs. Foul play is not suspected at this time. Anyone who may have witnessed the accident or has information as to next of kin is asked to contact the Gillford Police Department. The police are also asking for help in locating the woman's six-year-old daughter, Pearl Ann Wayland, who may be staying with friends.

I've learned by now that the location of this skimpy article in the newspaper screams that Nona Wayland didn't amount to a hill of beans and is hardly worth the space. Nona Wayland—a waitress at a honky-tonk dive with an address on lower Courtland Street where last-ditch poor whites live right next to the railroad tracks.

I read the notice over and over. There is no way I can see Nona Wayland dead. Her wild expression, her smeary red mouth, and the way her meaty body strained against that rumpled pink uniform are locked somewhere in my brain. Now she's become just a few lines at the bottom of a newspaper page that don't even take up as much space as the summer shoe-sale ad next to them.

People in town will cluck over her untimely end for a while, quoting "the wages of sin" and all that. Then from here on out, she'll be that trashy waitress who got drunk and fell down the stairs and broke her neck. That's all it's going to amount to for her. I try to picture her as a little girl. She was probably right pretty and full of sass. Now she's dead, and nobody is surprised. Or maybe even cares. Worst of all, her stupid death seems to have reduced Pearl Ann Wayland to little more than a missing puppy.

A Perfect Little Girl—
Friday Morning, August 15th

Mama took the bus into Savannah early this morning for her regular visit to Dr. Winslow for her "nervous condition." She left a note for me on the kitchen table saying that Bailey was going with her and that they'd be back late tonight. She won't go downtown to see Dr. Hopper because she says she doesn't want half the town knowing her business.

Ever since Francis died, she's had spells where she stays up half the night scrubbing and cleaning or baking. Sometimes she lays out dress patterns on some of her fabric yardage. She spreads this all over the living room floor, positioning each piece of tissue just so, as if her life depends on it. Once in a while she cuts the patterns out, but usually she doesn't. The next morning we fold the tissues and the fabric and put them away as if it's everyday normal. I don't know how she manages to hide all this restlessness when Daddy's home, but she does. Maybe he has a calming effect on her—or maybe she doubles up on the pills Dr. Winslow gives her.

I heard her on the telephone last night talking to that minister in Charleston, saying something about Bailey getting a physical exam. I don't know if she meant today or not, but at least he's with her and not here. Just the same, I have the front door locked and the latch on the kitchen screen door so I won't be thrown off if he shows up out of the blue. He's had this funny expression on his face ever since he heard about Nona Wayland's death, as though his skin is stretched too tight, while his eyelids keep blinking and blinking, and you get the feeling that his mind is racing a mile a minute.

I get up and pour myself another cup of coffee. It feels good to be home alone; I can have as many cups of coffee as I want. The house is quiet except for the steady ticktock of the clock on the living room mantel. Hanging on the wall above the clock is a big, gold-framed painting of the mighty clipper, the *Flying Cloud*. When Daddy's home, I often catch him stretched back in his easy chair, eyes almost closed but fixed upon the *Cloud*, and I know that somewhere deep inside himself he's pacing her deck, lifting his face to the salt spray.

It floors me that he's willing to live in Gillford, away from *his* ocean, just to please Mama, but more and more I'm beginning to see he doesn't know her nearly as well as he thinks he does. It's only the last couple of years that I've started thinking of them as people other than my parents. It gives me a funny feeling, even embarrassing at times. Deenie says her parents love each other just like in the movies. I'm not sure I believe that.

Before I know it, I'm mooning over John Howard. This is his volunteer day for yard work at the library. My books aren't due, but maybe Deenie and I can drop by this afternoon, and I can casually mention something about him stopping by last Monday. Too pushy, I decide, even though I know there will never be anyone else for me but John Howard Thompson.

There's a scratchy sound at the door as if something is nibbling through the screen. Pearl Ann Wayland is hunched over, peering into the kitchen.

"You got any more them baloney samiches?" Her voice rags off at the end.

Good Lord! I hurry to the door and hold it open for her. She's barefoot and dirty. Each side of her thin face is streaked from eyes to chin with the bleached-out tracks of dried tears.

"Here," I say, pulling out a chair from the table. "Sit here, and I'll make you a nice big baloney sandwich."

She pulls herself up onto the chair and runs the tips of her fingers over the spotless tablecloth in front of her. She's so flimsy, so twiggy, I keep thinking she'll disappear right in front of me. "You want some milk? With chocolate in it?" Her eyes widen, and her mouth drops open.

I sit quietly while she gobbles down the sandwich and drains the glass. I wonder when she last ate.

"You want a cookie?"

She watches me reach for the teddy bear cookie jar. I put two sugar cookies on the table in front of her. She studies them, then leans over and sniffs first one, then the other.

"Go ahead," I say, and she gingerly bites and chews her way through them.

"Did you know folks are looking for you?" I'm keeping my voice soft and even.

She shakes her head no.

"Did you get lost?" I ask. She doesn't answer. She's beyond tired, weary is what she is, and dirty. She hasn't been washed in a long time. "You know what?" I say. "Why don't I give you a bird bath in the sink, and then we can go sit in the living room and visit."

Her eyes brighten. "A bird bath?"

"Yeah, just like the birdies do—right up there in the sink. Ever see a bird take a bath?"

She shakes her head again.

When I come back with towels and soap, she's reaching up, trying to touch the picture of the puppies in a basket on front of the calendar. I pull a chair over to the sink and lift her up on it. She smells stale and pissy, and I turn my head aside.

"Let's take off this dress," I say, slowly pulling it over her head. She stands naked and motionless as I drop the filthy dress to the linoleum. "Maybe we can wash your hair, too? It always feels good when I wash mine." She doesn't say anything, just watches me soap up the washcloth.

Mama would keel over if she knew I was washing this grimy ragamuffin in her kitchen sink. The thought of her face if she walked in right now makes me giggle. Pearl Ann reaches up and pokes her finger into one of my dimples.

"That's a dimple," I say. "See, one on each side." And I give her my big dimple smile.

"Did somebody do that to you?"

"No," I say quickly. "Dimples run in families. My daddy's got them, too. He says they're angel kisses." She seems to like that. It's only after I've washed her arms and upper body that I notice the fading yellow bruises on her thin chest. I turn her around. Her shoulder blades stick out like wing nubbins. There's a dark purple bruise at her waist just to the left of her bony spine. Red welts splay across her narrow behind. She sees me looking at them.

"I'm a very bad girl," she says, ducking her head down.

I've never seen anything like this, and it flusters me. "You are? Who says that?"

"Mama." Her voice is resigned, little more than a sigh.

I throw a towel up on the counter and sit her up there. Her feet are black on the bottom, and dirt is ground in around her heels and in between her toes. I fill the sink with warm water. "Let's soak these piggies for a while." She gives me a puzzled look. "Your toes," I say. "Stick those piggies in the water."

She repeats it under her breath. "Piggies . . . stick those piggies in the water." I suds up the water to keep her occupied, but mostly to calm myself down.

"Can I have another one of them cookies when we're done?" She looks at me, crimping her mouth together.

"You can have the whole jar of cookies, Pearl Ann." I start to scrub her feet and can't hold back the rush of tears stinging my eyelids.

"Are you sad?" she asks.

"No, I got some soap in my eyes."

When I'm done, I wrap her in a towel and carry her upstairs to my bedroom.

"You won't forget my cookie, will you?" she whispers.

"No. I won't forget." I plop her down on the bed and get one of my old shirts for her. "Why don't you take a little nap? I'll be right here, and when you wake up, there'll be all the cookies you can eat."

She curls up on her side, and within minutes, she's fast asleep. I sit on the edge of the bed, watching her. I have never seen her smile. I lift her top lip with my finger—her two front teeth, ragged and almost transparent, are pushing through her inflamed gums. Her clean hair curls in wisps over her head. At first her breathing is shallow, then as she sinks into a deep sleep, it becomes slow and steady. I pick up one of her hands. Its fingers are long and slender, and the fingernails have been gnawed down to the quick. I tuck it up next to her cheek. She smells clean. Her lips part as she begins to snore softly. All along, underneath the layers of grime, was this perfect little girl. A knot of anger at dead Nona Wayland settles in my chest.

THE ROAR INSIDE MY HEAD—
Friday Afternoon, August 15th

I've pulled the shades against the late afternoon sun. The light in the bedroom is hazy and golden. The fan oscillating back and forth on the dresser riffles the edges of the voile curtains and skims over Pearl Ann's wispy hair. She's been sound asleep since a little past noon. She stirs once in a while but never wakes up. It's as if her body knows she's safe and has wrapped itself in a cocoon of sleep.

I told her I'd stay with her, and that's what I'm doing. To pass the time, I decided to tackle the big dog-eared copy of *Forever Amber* that Deenie sneaks from her mother's bedroom bookcase. She calls it *The Birds and Bees, Book One* because of all the racy scenes. It's been passed around in high school so much some of its pages are missing. Now, after three straight hours of reading, my eyelids are feeling gritty, and I laugh to myself—Mama would have a conniption fit if she knew I was reading this.

I get up, go rinse my face off in the bathroom, and bring the damp cloth back with me. Pearl Ann's face glistens with perspiration. She doesn't wake up when I wipe it off, but her eyelids flutter. Maybe she's dreaming a good dream. I know I should call the police and tell them she's here, but I can't bring myself to do it. What's to become of her now? What did she ever do to deserve being born to someone like Nona Wayland?

I settle back in my chair, and random thoughts flit back and forth across my mind. Bailey will be leaving soon, going to Charleston where some minister is going to help him find his way. Whatever that means. John Howard definitely hasn't forgotten about me. Daddy will be heading back home before long, and Mama will turn into his perfect wife again. I wonder what she'll tell him about Bailey. I have a feeling that he's never heard of Bailey Munroe.

The phone rings, rousing me from my reverie. I hurry downstairs, hoping maybe it's John Howard. It's not. It's Deenie, and her voice sounds stiff, choked back.

"What's wrong?" I ask.

"There's something going on down at the police station."

"Like what?"

"That Nona Wayland . . ."

"What about her?"

"Daddy got an anonymous phone call at the paper yesterday morning. A woman said she heard Nona Wayland arguing with a man right about the time . . . it happened."

"Yeah?"

"Then I heard Daddy telling Mama that Dr. Hopper took another look at the body and said suspicious bruises, like thumb marks, had shown up on her throat."

"Geez, Deenie, that's gruesome."

"Yeah, it is. He also told Mama that the police are thinking maybe somebody did it deliberately."

"You're serious?"

"Serious enough to tell him about that Bailey."

"What're you talking about?"

There's a pause. "I told Daddy what you said about your . . . about this Bailey . . . how strange you said he is, nutty, and how you don't think he's a veteran at all . . . that things don't add up."

"Why would you do that?" A wave of nausea hits my stomach, and I lean against the wall to steady myself.

Her words gush out, tumbling over each other. "Because we saw them together out at the Laughing Moon that day, and the way he shoved your bike, you could've fallen down, and he didn't even stop to see if you were hurt. . . ."

"My God, Deenie, I deliberately provoked him! You saw me do it!"

"I thought you wanted to get rid of him."

"I do, but not like this! Suppose this gets back to my mother!"

"I thought you were so scared of him!"

"I am!" I haven't told her that I keep my bedroom door locked, and I haven't told her about seeing him out at Hingle Creek, either. I usually tell her everything. Now I'm glad I didn't.

She doesn't say a word.

"I thought I could trust you." My voice sounds as if it's coming through a long tunnel. "Suppose this gets back to my mother! How could you do this to me . . . especially now!"

I can hear little squeaking noises, and I know she's trying not to cry.

"He's Mama's brother, for God's sake, and he's . . . he's got problems, but he doesn't go around killing women! He's just . . . I told you those things in confidence, Deenie! He's going to be leaving in a few days."

Silence settles between us.

"Afton?" she says.

"What's done is done," I say, "but do me a favor. Tell your father that you exaggerated, that I was the one mad and provoked Bailey. Tell him that he's getting help. Someone in Charleston is going to be helping him. He's leaving!"

"Oh, Afton." She sounds as if she's choking on tears.

"What?"

"They're going to—"

Suddenly, I hear Mr. Mason's voice in the background. "Who're you talking to?" There's a click, and the line goes dead.

I think I hear a whimper from upstairs, but when I reach my bedroom, Pearl Ann is still sleeping. I walk over to the bed to see if she's all right. Her breathing is even and steady, but I can't hear it because of the roar inside my head.

SCARCELY BREATHING—
Friday Night, August 15th

Mama's face is a wreck, grief and disbelief twisting her small, even features almost beyond recognition. I've managed to get her to the kitchen table and ease her down to a chair. I get the new bottle of prescription pills from her purse, and with hands shaking so badly I'm splashing water from the glass all over the place, I get two pills down her throat. She lays her head on her arms, and I massage her hunched shoulders. Little by little the pills begin to do their work, and she slowly relaxes.

Deputy Warren was waiting for their bus in from Savannah tonight, she says. The minute Bailey stepped off, Warren said they'd like to talk with him down at the police station. No, he wasn't under arrest—they just wanted to talk with him about something. Mrs. Hudson heard all of this and came to Mama's aid and drove her home, but had to leave her at the front door because Mama wouldn't let her in the house.

She raises her head and sits up. Her face is blank. "What is this all about?" she says to herself. I have to strain to hear her. "Who found out?" She looks at me. "Who would do this to him?" she asks. I shake my head and look away quickly. "I don't understand," she says. "Do you know what this is about?"

I touch her arm. "It's about that Nona Wayland." My voice is shaky.

Her eyebrows pucker together. "Nona Wayland? What's that got to do with Bailey?"

"The police think maybe it wasn't an accident."

She stops and looks at me hard, and I hear this funny crooning sound coming from the back of her throat.

"Someone saw the two of them all lovey-dovey coming out of the Laughing Moon last week."

"The Laughing Moon?" She repeats it as if trying to understand some foreign language. "Oh. You mean that honky-tonk?"

She tips her face up toward the ceiling, wavers for an instant, and then slides off her chair to the floor as if all her bones had suddenly melted inside her.

She comes to quickly, and I help her back to the chair. She's moaning softly. "Someone found out," she's saying. "Oh, dear Lord, someone found out." She looks up at me. "What do I do now? I've ruined us. Charles will never forgive me."

What is she saying? That she knows Bailey had something to do with Nona Wayland's death? I feel the hairs go up on my arms.

"Mama, Daddy will forgive you anything, you know that," I say, reaching for her hand across the table. "Whatever it is."

"No." She shakes her head. "I'm Job's daughter, cursed, and I don't know why."

She means old Job in the Bible, going through one plague after the other until there was hardly anything left of him. "Don't say that, Mama."

She pulls her hand away. "Why didn't they wait till tomorrow and talk to him on the front porch?" She thinks that over. "Somebody found out," she says. "Why else were they waiting for him so late at night, wanting him to go down to the police station?"

I hear myself asking, "What did someone find out, Mama?"

She studies her hands for so long, stroking her fingernails, each in turn, that I think she hasn't heard me.

"Mama, please. Please tell me."

She sits up straighter and studies my face.

"Please," I say.

"He hasn't been in a military hospital since the war." She's watching me, trying to gauge my reaction.

I'm sitting still, but my skin feels like it's crawling. "He's . . ."

"He's what, Mama?"

"He's been in prison." Her voice is almost inaudible.

"You mean . . . *prison?*"

"Get Charlotte's angel for me," she says.

"Mama?"

"Just get it."

I bring the figurine in and set it on the table in front of her. She turns it over and peels off the oval of green felt on its base. I draw back, half expecting to see Charlotte's little spirit come sailing out. Instead, Mama pokes her finger up through the hole in the bottom. I can't believe it! She has something hidden inside it! How much stuff does she have hidden around this house, anyway? She works out a small yellowing roll of newsprint. I watch, fascinated, as she spreads open the paper. Its edges keep curling in, so she turns it over and rolls it up the reverse way until it flattens. Then she slides it across the table toward me. It's dated April 18, 1925.

There is a grainy picture of Bailey, tall and skinny, his head hanging down, his hands cuffed behind him, and two burly men with deputy badges on their lapels scowling on either side of him. The headline reads *Munroe Sentenced in Miss Winton's Death.* Underneath the picture it says, *Bailey Reid Munroe, 18, of Clanton Spring was given a sentence today of fifteen years to life at hard labor for the wrongful death of 17-year-old Susan Marie Winton, the daughter of Douglas and Mildred Winton of Clanton Spring and the granddaughter of Circuit Court Judge Hayland Winton. Mrs. Winton fainted during the sentencing and was carried from the courtroom. Judge Winton was heard to remark later on the courthouse steps that if he has anything to do with it, Munroe will never walk free again. He said he doubted that Munroe was man enough to survive Tuckman Penal Farm. When asked about the Munroe family charges that they're being harassed by nightriders, Judge Winton said he knows nothing about that, but it might be a good idea for the Munroes to make themselves scarce in Clanton Spring.*

I read it several times, trying to get it through my head. I even turn it over as though some explanation will be there along with the price of chicken feed in the advertisement on the back. I read the name over and over. Susan Winton. Susan. The paper in my hand is shaking—that's the name Bailey yelled over and over out at Hingle Creek. *Susan.* He killed her?

Mama breaks the silence. "I put it inside the angel so she'd maybe look out for him. Charlotte. Maybe she'd look out for him."

Is she serious? That *don't dare touch it* china angel has been standing on the mantel for years! I remember the morning I came downstairs and found Bailey sitting in Daddy's chair holding the angel, neither of us knowing that his secret was inside. It seems too outlandish, like something out of a movie, not something that happens in real life. The air in the kitchen is thick, almost stifling, yet the chill running along my spine is cold as ice.

He's a killer? I've thought a lot of bad things about him, but never this. My hands tremble as I ease the newspaper clipping back across the table. I push away from the table and try to take a deep breath. Once a killer, always a killer, that's what the farmers say about the renegade wild dogs that stalk livestock. And Nona Wayland? I think I'm going to throw up.

"Afton . . ."

"How could you not tell me, Mama?" The question hangs in the air like a hornet's needle.

She just stares at me.

"How could you not tell me!" I'm almost yelling now.

"Look at you," she says. "Just look at you! You think I didn't see from the first day that you didn't like him!" She spreads her hands out on the table in front of her. "How in the name of God would you have treated him if I'd told you this? I think we both know, don't we?"

"Maybe Nona Wayland would still be alive . . ."

She gasps. "You think he killed that woman—because of this?" She grabs the newspaper clipping and pushes it up in my face. "He didn't murder Susan Winton! They made a suicide pact when her family called a halt to things because he wasn't good enough. Her grandfather, Judge Winton, was a mean old buzzard."

Suicide pact? I feel as though I've been punched in the stomach, but my mind won't let go of blaming Mama for shutting me out.

"I don't care!" I blurt out. "You should've told me! You owed me the truth!"

"I did? Why is that? You have no idea what he's been through. None! You're always so sure you're right about everything."

The blood is coming back into her face; her eyes are blinking the way they do when she's becoming angry.

"But how could you let people think he was a war veteran—"

She stops me cold. "Don't start in on that with me! Do you know how people treat men from the penal farms? Why do you think old Tommy Black is such a drunk? Because he spent five years on the chain gang for stealing a chicken? No, because after he came home, people treated him like dirt, worse than scum, worse than the lowest thing that ever crawled on the face of the earth. Dirty. Unfit."

Suddenly, she's sobbing, her head again buried in her arms on the table. Her voice is muffled and anguished. "I'm not saying what he did was right, but he paid for it in the worst way possible . . . worse even than the prison farm. You have no idea."

Her words are slowly beginning to get past my anger and sink in. A suicide pact? Is it like that story some of the old folks still shake their heads over? About the boy and girl found in a barn years and years ago, dead of poison, the bottle still in his hand, and no one ever knew where they came from or why they did it?

I look at her. Her breathing is ragged as she tries to check her crying and calm herself.

"What happened, Mama? What did they do?"

"They drove Papa's truck to the upper pasture just after daybreak, then said their prayers and headed full tilt for Devil's Boulder. That's where it happened— Devil's Boulder." Her shoulders shudder. "After the trial, just before they took him away, he told me that he wished they'd go ahead and hang him. He said he couldn't get Susan's face out of his mind."

Her sobs burst loose again, raising goose bumps on my arms. "He said she'd changed her mind at the last minute—she wanted out. He tried to put on the brakes. Instead the truck slammed sideways into the boulder, throwing him clear but crushing all the life out of her."

Part of me feels her terrible pain, but part of me is angry beyond belief with her. How could she lie to me about this? *It wasn't really a lie,* she says. *I was just trying to protect both of you.* What does she mean—it wasn't a lie? A lie doesn't have to be bald faced. A lie is looking people dead in the eye when they think one thing and letting them believe what you know is a lie.

She raises her head; her face is beginning to puff up, her eyes are bleary with tears. "All I wanted was to give him a little start, a place to feel safe, get on his feet, until he went out on his own . . . all I asked of you was to just let him be for a while." She sits up, reaches for a paper napkin, and blows her nose. We fall quiet again, then she says in a kind of dreamlike remembering, "Mama and Papa disowned him. They went to their graves with their hearts set against him. After my sister Essie's sweetheart up and called off their wedding a couple of weeks later, both my sisters, Essie and Marla, turned their backs on Bailey, trying to separate themselves from what he did."

She's crying softly again. "The shame was so awful. I never expected to see him again in this lifetime."

I don't like seeing her like this, but I don't know how to stop it, and I'm not sure I even want to.

"So few get off those prison farms alive, and if they do, they're hardly human anymore." She blows her nose again and wipes her eyes with the heels of her hands. "I didn't ask you to love him, Afton. . . ."

"I don't love Mr. Bonney no more." Pearl Ann is standing in the kitchen doorway. Mama is startled. She looks back and forth from Pearl Ann to me.

"It's Pearl Ann Wayland," I say. "I washed her."

Pearl Ann walks over to me and lays her hand on my shoulder.

"Is your mama hurt?"

"Yes," I murmur.

"Mr. Bonney hurt my mama."

Both Mama and I are staring at her as she eyes the cookie jar. "Is my cookie in there?" she asks.

I WANT TO SCRUB ALL OF THIS OFF—
Thursday, August 21st

I surprised myself, hurting deep down inside the way I did after the police left with Pearl Ann last Saturday morning. When they came for her, she stood so close to me that anybody could see she didn't want to go, but she didn't make a fuss at all. I asked where they'd be taking her. To the County Children's Home, they said. I emptied the cookie jar into my old Mickey Mouse lunchbox and gave it to her. She waved good-bye from the car, already eating one of her cookies. Pearl Ann Wayland and I haven't seen the last of each other; we're connected somehow.

Everyone's talking about Walter Bonney, how Pearl Ann told what she saw the night her mother died, how he turned himself in when the manhunt for him spread out from Gillford. You'd have thought they were on the trail of some hard-boiled old gangster like John Dillinger instead of a little fat man who surrendered with his hands way up over his head, they say, crying like a baby.

The story is that he kept asking Nona Wayland if Pearl Ann could go live with his sister in Oaklee. On that last night they got to arguing about it, going up the stairway to her place. He said she finally offered to *sell* Pearl Ann for three hundred dollars, and he was so shocked, he went berserk and hit her, and she fell down the stairs. But folks are already adding their two cents, shaking their heads and saying there's more to it than that. I overheard a couple of women at Kirk's Dixie Mart saying, "To think that man was in my kitchen!" Stuff like that. We'll probably never know for sure what really happened, but before it's over and done with, Walter Bonney will be the monster that stalked Gillford.

I don't know how long I've been sitting here at my bedroom window, staring out into the deepening night. It's quiet except for an occasional hoot of a night owl. The low-riding moon is shooting slivers of silver through the magnolia onto the lawn. Every once in a while, a moth or beetle hits the screen, crawls along steadying itself, then takes off again. A swarm of fireflies lifts suddenly from the bushes where the old dog, my Traveler, camped out. As I watch them dance in the air, I'm struggling to understand the way life can change in the blink of an eye.

About an hour ago, Mr. Mason's station wagon pulled up across the street in front of Auntie Mason's. Deenie and her parents got out. She glanced up at my window before following them through the gate. I haven't talked with her since her phone call last week—and I miss her.

The radio console downstairs goes quiet, and I hear Mama and Bailey head back to the kitchen. What are they saying to each other?

Last night after supper something hit the front porch. Bailey stepped out and came back with a rock wrapped in paper. I stood in the living room archway and watched him unwrap the paper and read it. He had absolutely no expression on his face. He just stood there, staring down at it. Then he saw me and walked toward me. I drew back, more afraid of him than ever. He killed his sweetheart; it's as simple as that. He talked her into something she really didn't want to do. I didn't like him from the minute I first saw him, and I don't like him now. I'll never like him. He stopped and held the paper out to me. I shook my head no. Then he read it aloud in a hesitating way.

"Jailbird, go back to where you come from."

Mama came up behind me, brushed past, and took the paper from him.

"I'm going to call Reverend Lovejoy," she said, "and see if we can't . . ." She looked up at Bailey. "It's going to be all right, you'll see."

He pulled the paper from her fingers, folded it over and over, and tucked it in his shirt pocket. "I messed it up for you, didn't I?" he said to her.

Their reactions were identical—sagging shoulders, nervous hands, faces wearing expressions of sorrow for each other. For just a second they seemed like the distorted images you see in those trick mirrors at the carnival. I couldn't bear to watch them, and I went on upstairs to my bedroom that's beginning to feel more and more like my prison.

I want to take a bath. I want to scrub all of this off me, but I don't want to open my door and run the risk of having to look at either of them. While I'm trying to make up my mind, there's a soft tapping at my door. It's not Mama's tapping. I sit silently. Maybe he'll think I'm asleep. But, no, there it is again. His raspy voice seeps through the door.

"Afton?"

I pad over to the door, listening. I can hear him breathing.

"Can I tell you something?"

My curiosity gets the better of me. "What?" I ask.

"You gonna open the door?"

I know I'm not going to open the door.

"Listen . . . Afton . . . I was just a wrongheaded boy . . . all bollixed up . . . I loved that girl." He's having a hard time getting his words out, and I'm wondering if he's ever said them out loud before. "I did a terrible thing. I'm the one should've died in that wreck—and I reckon maybe I did, 'cause I'll never be free of it." He waits for me to say something. When I don't, he goes on back downstairs.

I hardly sleep at all, rousing every hour or so, and whenever I do, I hear them moving around downstairs. Once I think I hear an automobile in the driveway. Toward dawn, I jolt awake from a dream of fog spiraling through the house, someone crying in the closet under the stairs, and Charlotte's angel beckoning from the mantel, its wings chipped and stained with blood.

People Can Be So Cruel—
Tuesday, August 26th

Bailey has been gone for five days now. The night he tried to talk with me through my bedroom door—that was probably his way of saying good-bye. When he was gone in the morning, I was glad. I keep hearing Deenie's voice the last time I talked with her on the telephone. "Well, you wanted to get rid of him, didn't you?" But it happened in such an awful way. Why couldn't I have liked him just a little? I'm not sorry he's gone. I feel bad for Mama, though.

She's retreated so far into herself, she hardly knows I'm here at times. If she could fold herself up and slip in between the floorboards or hide behind the wallpaper, I think she'd do it. Her face is blotched and puffy, but she doesn't cry in front of me anymore. We dust and clean, we work in the victory garden, we shell beans and put up tomatoes, but she's doing it all by rote. I do the shopping. I answer the telephone and the doorbell. If anyone asks for her, I say she's not feeling well today.

She thinks someone zeroed in on Bailey and deliberately did him in. I caught her the other day at the front window watching Auntie Mason working in her garden.

"Do you think it was the Masons?" she said. My knees faltered, and I grabbed the sofa arm and sat down. "No, Mama, it wasn't the Masons. Auntie Mason loves you."

"Who, then?" She turned her head and looked at me. "Who could be so cruel? I had no idea I had such a *cruel* enemy."

"It wasn't you, Mama. Maybe they just didn't want Bailey around." I realize I've said too much, but she doesn't follow through. I don't think she even heard me.

It's more than Bailey, though. It's Daddy, too. She looks at me now over our tuna sandwiches and out of the blue says, "Charles is bound to hear about this. Whoever did this will make sure he finds out. How will I ever explain it to him?"

"It's not all that bad, Mama." I almost cringe at my words. If the whole town isn't chewing on this day and night, I'm a monkey's uncle.

"I tried to see Bailey once . . . at that place . . . before I married Charles . . . but they wouldn't even let me get off the bus. The driver told me that I should just consider Bailey dead, go home and have a funeral and be done with it." She sets her sandwich down and picks at it with her fingers. "What an awful thing to say."

Her voice rises and falls softly, and I can't take my eyes off her. "There was an old woman on that bus, took my name and address, and wrote down Bailey's name. Her husband was a pastor. She said he had a nephew working at the prison. I remember she patted my hand and said they'd hold me in their prayers. Pastor Locke wrote every year or two, letting me know that Bailey was still alive. It stopped during the war. I figure the old man died." She gives me a pinched smile.

"There's a reason why somebody went out of their way to snoop and snoop and snoop until they . . ." She pushes her chair back, stands up, and begins clearing off the table.

"I'll do that," I say.

She heads toward the hallway, then stops and looks back.

"Can you imagine the cruelty of someone going out of their way to hurt him like that after all he's been through? Just a few more days, and he'd have been on his way with Reverend Lovejoy. Just a few—" She stops in midsentence, and an odd expression settles on her face. "Do you suppose it's somehow connected with him? The letters . . . maybe someone at the post office . . ."

She's not going to let any of this go anytime soon. "No, Mama," I say. "It wasn't anyone at the post office."

She gives me a look. "You don't know that." There's a long pause as she stares at me. "Or do you?"

I glance away from her, a bitter taste filling my mouth. Is this what guilt tastes like?

"Afton? Did you have anything to do with this? You said you were afraid of him. But you have to know in your heart how . . . harmless he is, don't you? Tell me you didn't air your grievances outside the house . . . with anyone."

She means Deenie. She's waiting for me to say something, standing in the doorway, hugging herself as if to keep her hurt from spilling out all over the floor.

How can I tell her that yes, I'm the culprit? That I set him up as surely as if I'd done it deliberately. I want to go through the floor; I can't bear the look on her face.

"My God, Mama, no! No, I'd never hurt you like this!" Tears sting my eyelids and slide down my face.

She's instantly at my side. "I'm sorry, Afton. I didn't mean it . . . I didn't mean it." She has her arms around me.

"It's all right, Mama." I cringe at the high-minded tone of forgiveness in my voice. I can't believe I'm letting her take the brunt of it.

I put on a pot of coffee, and we sit at the table again. Her hands are folded in her lap, and she's shaking her head slowly as if something inside can't believe the turn of things.

"I'm going to break Charles's heart. He's going to wonder why I didn't love him enough to trust him."

When your mother suddenly talks to you as an adult about her faults, not yours, you're entering into dangerous territory. I look down at the table so she can't see my expression.

"Do you think I'm terrible, Afton?"

I shake my head no.

"When you're eighteen and suddenly on your own, how do you tell people that your twin brother is on a penal farm for killing his sweetheart? That is the worst kind of prison there is. I tried at first, but people can be so cruel. The looks on their faces . . . it was awful. Your twin? The person who came into this world with you? Bad blood—doubled. Then they'd look away, leaving me feeling tainted, ruined even."

She sighs and pushes her hair back off her forehead. "My family wasn't very loving. When this happened, we scattered like straws in the wind as though we couldn't bear to look at each other. It was finally easier to just say they'd all been wiped out by scarlet fever. Funny thing was, after a while I almost believed it myself."

We sit quietly for a long time, sipping our coffee and not really looking at each other. I keep hearing her voice from last Friday night saying, "I'm cursed, and I don't know why."

When the mantel clock in the living room chimes the hour, she stands and carefully pushes her chair to the table.

"Let's just keep all of this to ourselves," she says. "If you'll clear off the table and clean up in here, I can do some sewing before *Ma Perkins* comes on." Right before my eyes she's slipped back inside her old skin. I'm not sure she'll ever talk with me about this again.

I finish up in the kitchen and give it one last check before leaving. I spy Charlotte's angel behind the cookie jar as if it's hiding. It doesn't belong there; it belongs on the living room mantel. When I pick it up, I can't resist turning it over, but there's no felt oval, no hidden newspaper clipping inside. Charlotte's angel is free of its terrible secret. Carrying it back into the living room, its reality stings me—my sister, Charlotte, was a real person. Mama grew her, birthed her, and seven days later, lost her. The words *woman of sorrows* billow inside my head. It sounds like something from a poem I've read, but I can't remember.

I ease down into the security of Daddy's overstuffed chair and study the figurine, back in its place on the mantel. When they laid Baby Charlotte to rest, Mama had no idea that in just a few more years, the little boy at her side would be gone, too. It strikes me that I've never ever thought of that before, and a painful knot sticks in my throat.

The sewing machine stops, and her footsteps sound in the hallway. I get up and turn on the radio; I'll listen to *Ma Perkins* with her. Her footsteps quicken when she hears the theme music. And suddenly I know why she clings to them—they'll never leave her.

WE ARE ALL WE HAVE LEFT—
Friday, August 29th

I call Deenie this morning and ask her if she wants to take the bus into Savannah with me tomorrow and shop around for new school clothes. We're subdued, no doubt about it, but neither of us mentions Bailey or what happened. It's good to hear her voice, and pretty soon things get more lighthearted. We wind up talking about what we'll wear tomorrow so we don't clash. Maybe one of these days, when we're old and gray, I'll tell her how much I missed her.

I check through my clothes closet; nothing looks good. When I pull my peasant blouse from its hanger and flip it toward the bed, it sideswipes the dresser and sends my gold locket skittering across the floor. I pick it up and, out of habit, open it. There's Francis. It feels as if someone just dropped a wet towel on my head. I close my hand around the locket. I'm going to miss him for the rest of my life. Every joy, every sorrow, I'll wish he were here to celebrate with me or console me. I walk over to the window.

The morning sunlight dancing through the glossy leaves of the old magnolia plays a trick on me. Sitting high up on a branch, swinging his legs, dangling my Betsy Wetsy doll by one foot and daring me to come up after it, is a memory of twelve-year-old Francis Dupree. And then it hits me so hard I feel as though my heart might burst.

Mama loves Bailey the way I love Francis.

She probably thought he was dead. Then she looked up one day, and there he was again. I try to imagine how I'd feel if I looked across my room, and suddenly Francis was standing in the doorway. All she wanted to do was give him a chance, breathing space, a way to figure out how to fit back in—a way to be part of her life again. She failed. She couldn't protect him from me. I can blame her all I want—you know, if she hadn't done *this*, I wouldn't have done *that*—but it won't change a thing, because he didn't survive me.

Daddy will be home before Thanksgiving. We're both waiting for him—he makes us a family again. But this time it'll be different, and the minute he walks into the house, he'll sense it.

Mama has to figure out a way to tell him about her brother, Bailey, and how their plans blew up in their faces. She's kept so much from Daddy for so many years, I don't think she even knows how to go about that. In her mind, someone in town caught her in her own web of secrecy and deceit—a web she's been spinning most of her life. She'll never be able to look into any face around here again without wondering if it's the one.

How can I let her spend the rest of her life like that?

I had the chance last Tuesday to admit that if I hadn't dumped all my bad feelings about Bailey on Deenie, probably none of this would have happened. She asked me point-blank if I had anything to do with it. I surprised myself by how quickly and easily I lied. *No! No! No! I'd never hurt you like that!* I've only made it worse.

I step into the hallway. I'll go downstairs and tell her that it was me who shoved Bailey into the spotlight. My stomach feels like a hurricane is going on inside. I walk to the head of the stairway. I lay my hand on the rail and try to force myself to take the first step down, but I don't budge. I can't do it! I turn and hurry back to my bedroom.

I catch sight of myself in the mirror. It brings me up short. I look different somehow—around the eyes. What's that all about? I lean toward the mirror, staring at my face. Hypocrite. That's what comes to mind. I've been so busy this year building up criticism and resentment for all of her half-truths and evasions, and here I'm doing the same thing, only mine is an outright lie.

All I had to do was say, "Yes, Mama, I said terrible things about Bailey. I didn't want him here. But if I'd known it would turn out like this . . ." She'd be furious with me, but she'd be free of thinking some self-righteous high and mighty was bent on punishing her and Bailey. Instead, I did what she's done for years—I tried to cover my tracks.

Is this how it starts? Without warning, something you do brings the house crashing down around your ears, and you can't bear the thought of it, much less owning up to it. Deenie says she can build a scenario to cover any of her sins right on the spot, and before long she starts to believe it herself. Even if I could go down that road, it's not what I want. Knowing me, I'd be forever dipping and dodging and trying not to slip up. I want to be me, out in the open, take me or leave me, just as I am.

I walk round and round my room. I need to go downstairs and tell her, but just thinking about her hurt and anger is giving me the shakes. Is she feeling that way about Daddy, I wonder? How will she ever get up the nerve to tell him? When she mentions his name now, her lips tremble slightly, and her eyes widen as though she's trying to see into the bottom of a pit. I can't get that look out of my mind. Why did all of this have to happen, anyway? Why couldn't Bailey Munroe have just stayed out of our lives?

Auntie Mason says there's always the other side of the coin. Well, what's on the other side of all this? I can't think of anything good that's come from it— except—now I probably know my mother better than anyone else ever has. Is that a good thing? Maybe she'll push me farther away than ever.

I sit down on the window seat and leaf aimlessly through the *Ladies' Home Journal,* but I don't see a thing on the pages. Instead, there's a whisper of something drifting across my mind—a whisper that's saying *of course there's a reason.*

Am I the one who can finally help her—by showing her that I trust her to love me—in spite of myself?

Can I really show her the way?

"Francis," I whisper, "please help me." I slowly sink to my knees. "Help me, Lord, please. We're all that's left of our family—all that is left." I wait.

There's no miraculous flash of light, no angel wings rushing in the corner, no arms reaching out for me. But there is a tingling in my chest, a lightness that gradually spreads throughout my body until I feel as if I am cushioned on air.

SHE'S IN HER SEWING ROOM. She's finally making up one of her patterns. It's a jacket for me. We bought the fabric last year in Charleston. She doesn't hear me at first. Then she senses my presence and turns. "This is really your color," she says, holding up the basted garment. It's a deep, rich burgundy. "It'll set off your complexion to perfection."

"Mama?" I say, and she lowers the garment to her lap, resting her hands on top of it. Daddy loves her beautiful hands. She looks so tired.

"Yes?"

I move to her side quickly, kneel by her chair, and press my face against the half-sewn jacket on her lap. She's surprised. I hear the sharp intake of her breath, then she curves her hand over the top of my head and strokes my hair.

My eyes burn, my throat is on fire. But inside, there is a lightness.

I look up at her. "Mama," I say softly, "I have something to tell you."